The
Unsolvable
Circus

David J. Horn

Published in the United States by Horn Publishing.

ISBN: 978-0-6151-5193-9

Front cover art is a modification of a photograph, *Vellecita's Leopards* (1906).

The Unsolvable Circus

Table of Contents

*To Patricia for her patience
and Dino for his persistence*

Stealing Angie Quagmire

L ong gone were the legendary days of Edgar P. Allen's youth. As a young man his criminal exploits had made him something of a celebrity among the local community of crooks and cons. There was seemingly nothing he couldn't steal. He had even once, in order to win a bar bet, stole a priest from a church. But one evening Edgar's glory was snuffed out abruptly. As the police slapped the handcuffs on his wrists and read him his rights, Edgar had the uncanny feeling that nothing would ever be the same again. He entered prison at the age of 23, and when the doors opened again he was an old, old man.

On the day that Edgar was released from prison, he shuffled out of the great iron doors and into the bright pale sunlight. He stopped and peered about, shielding the the sunlight from his eyes with his hand. As he continued to shuffle his way out of the prison yard, past the tall electrified fences topped with barbed wire, his thoughts fluttered back to the last day he was a free man. He was in a court of law, charged with the murder of his best friend.

Although Edgar always insisted he was innocent, the State had proved he had a motive: the victim was having an affair with his young and voluptuous wife. The State also proved that the murder weapon belonged to Edgar and, unfortunately for Edgar, he had no alibi. Things looked discouragingly bleak.

But Edgar's lawyer, Samuel Weezel, was a firecracker. He was also an optimist, and he would coach Edgar along by telling him, "We have those bastards right where we want them." Edgar didn't share his lawyer's outlook, but he found it reassuring that Weezel wasn't ready to throw in the towel.

Weezel had originally wanted to call Edgar's two year old son to the stand. He imagined the child's tear jerking testimony. The whole court would sob and moan as the boy confessed his love for his daddy. But the boy proved to be a brat. It was nearly impossible to keep him seated and focused for longer than 15 seconds, and he usually answered Weezel's questions with embarrassing remarks about "poo poo" and "pee pee."

Seeing that the boy was of no use, Weezel turned his sights on Edgar. He didn't believe that he could prove Edgar was innocent, but he could get the jury to sympathize with the young man. How would he do this? He would call Edgar to the stand and paint a picture of Edgar's "horrifyingly abusive" childhood that would have the jury weeping for him. Not only would they find Edgar innocent, they would probably want to take him out for drinks after the trial. The fact that Edgar did not come from a "horrifyingly abusive" household didn't stop Weezel. He invented a story, and he and Edgar rehearsed a set of questions and answers.

As it was mentioned earlier, Samuel Weezel was a firecracker. He was a fine lawyer by all measures...when he was sober, and Samuel Weezel had been painfully sober for the entire trial, but as things began to wind down he also began to drink. A shot here, a beer there. The day that Edgar was called to the stand, Weezel was viciously drunk from the night before.

As Edgar sat in the witness box, Weezel paced unevenly up and down the courtroom. Before he began questioning Edgar, he winked at him. Weezel began by asking, "Edgar can you tell the court a little about your father? Was he a loving man?"

"No, sir. He was an abusive man."

"What did he do for a living?"

"Well, he was a car..."

"Your father, did he own a puppet theater for children? Let me rephrase. Did he own the *Pussy Cat Pandemonium* puppet theater for children?" Edgar was confused. This was not part of the script. But he reasoned that he had to follow Weezel's lead. So, he responded doubtfully, "Yes."

"And did he own the puppets for the play *Faust*?" Weezel asked as he zigzagged about the courtroom.

"Objection your honor. The State does not understand what a puppet theater owned by the defendant's father has to do with the murder of Mr. Henry," complained the D.A. jumping to his feet.

Weezel stopped at the D.A.'s table and whispered, "You arrogant son of a bitch. I'll take you out back and shove a live rat from the dumpster up your..."

"Mr. Weezel, please get to the point," urged the Judge who was oblivious to the threat Weezel had just made to the D.A.

"The point is your honor, that Mr. Allen spent his childhood in a puppet theater suspiciously named *Pussy Cat Pandemonium,* and that every Sunday my client would be subject to a spectacle of drunken puppetry by a man that stank like public urinal. A man that called himself a puppeteer, yet he only owned four puppets: Mephistopheles, Satan, Faust and the Pope." Weezel turned to the jury and sobbed dramatically, "Imagine a childhood where every Sunday a young boy would have to witness an improvised puppet show where Faust and the Pope would eventually find themselves dragged off to hell." The jury members glanced at one another wondering if any of the others understood what Weezel was talking about.

"Did he ever beat you with those puppets?" Weezel asked pointedly.

"Yes," responded Edgar quietly.

Weezel spun and faced the jury. He moved close to the jury box. He lowered his head and stood silently for a moment. Looking up he said, "You tell me who's to blame for this murder, Mr. Allen or his screwball father with his water glass full of gin and his 4 puppets, two of which were residents of hell?"

The jury answered this question a couple hours later by finding Edgar guilty of the crimes he was accused. Not one jury member felt even the smallest smidge of sympathy for Edgar. As a matter of fact, most members of the jury felt strangely repulsed by Edgar and his childhood spent in the suspiciously named, and completely fictional, *Pussy Cat Pandemonium.* Weezel's tactic had failed miserably.

Edgar's New Home

Once released from prison, Edgar lived with his grandson and grandson's family. His grandson, Gerry, had visited him a few times in jail because (he had explained to Edgar the first time he visited) he always wanted to meet his family members, no matter if they were murderers or not. Maybe Gerry's interest in his grandfather was due to the fact that he had been brought up to believe that his own father was the product of a miraculous birth: he had been conceived without the aid of a man. But as young Gerry matured and as he entered the age of reason, he began to doubt that his own father was in fact fatherless. So, he began searching for his father's father. He looked into the past and found Edgar, in the present, sitting in a prison cell, reading Shakespeare.

So, when Edgar was released from prison, Gerry was there to take him to his home. Gerry was nervous about the prospect of a convicted murderer living with him, no matter how old he was, but he reasoned that Edgar was family and he needed help; therefore, he felt obligated to do something for him. So, he dutifully and begrudgingly picked up the old man and drove him to his home.

But as the days passed, Gerry and his wife, Dawn, grew weary of Edgar and his constant complaining and cursing. It was clear that Edgar was simply a miserable old man who felt that he had been cheated out of his life. Gerry and Dawn did their best to try to pretend that they enjoyed Edgar's company, but they were not at all happy about having the old man about. Edgar was not a very congenial house guest, and it was obvious that he detested his grandson.

Gerry owned a fledgling courier service and this was all that he was capable of talking about. He would talk for hours about how big his fleet of vehicles was, how many vehicles he planned to have in two years, how the prices of gas were impacting his business, etcetera. Edgar found the enterprise of moving a package from one place to another dead boring. But he also found Gerry's business as a sign of weakness. Gerry preferred the life of low risk and little profit. He had no guts.

One night at supper, Gerry announced to Dawn and Edgar, "I've been thinking Gramps," Edgar cringed whenever Gerry reminded him that they were related, "that you could come work for me. You could get out of the house a couple hours a day and come down to the shop. What do you think?"

Edgar was as silent as a shark circling an unsuspecting swimmer.

"That would be a great idea," said Dawn encouragingly.

"How about it?" asked Gerry as he shoveled another forkful of mashed potatoes into his mouth.

"What would my job be?" asked Edgar with feigned politeness.

"You'd be a janitor. You know, mop the floors, clean the toilets, that sort of stuff."

Edgar gently placed his knife and fork on the table and said smiling, "I'd rather wipe the asses of the chimps in the zoo."

Gerry did not take this well. "That can be arranged," he said throwing his napkin down as he left the table.

Later that night, a tearful Dawn told Gerry, "Either the old man goes or I go," and then locked herself in the bathroom. So, Gerry, like a good husband but a bad grandson, planned the exit of his progenitor.

And so it was that one evening, only a few days after the conversation about Edgar's employment, Edgar fell asleep in his bed watching an episode of *Fear Factor,* and when he woke up he found himself in a strange bed, in a strange room, surrounded by strangers.

Dr. Harry Quagmire

As Edgar's eyes opened, one of the strangers began to address him, "Hello Mr. Allen, my name is Dr. Harry Quagmire, and I am here

12

to inform you that you are the newest member of our ever growing community of old farts." The group of strangers standing behind Dr. Harry Quagmire collectively let out a suppressed laugh.

"Just joking Mr. Allen," Dr. Quagmire placed a pointed party hat on Edgar's head. "Congratulations Mr. Allen, and welcome to your new home. The Relax Palace!" He said the words *Relax Palace* with such dramatic emphasis that a young nurse standing behind the doctor actually swooned.

Dr. Quagmire was a tall, handsome man. He had electric blue eyes and blond hair. It was his dashing looks that had helped him win a spot on the cover of the *Geriatric Care* medical journal. On the cover, he was pictured leaning towards a citizen of the Relax Palace, in a manner similar to a saint leaning into a sinner to dispense salvation. The only difference was that Dr. Quagmire, with his perfectly parted hair and his customary impatient and frigid gaze, did not appear to be a particularly compassionate nor sympathetic man. The doctor argued the opposite, however. He believed that the photo captured the essence of his caring and servitude. In reality though, the patient, Henry Tittles, whose voice had been reduced to a whisper over the years, was inaudibly rasping, "Hey asshole, you're blocking my view." It seemed that the doctor's photo-op was obstructing Henry's viewing of his favorite TV show, *Serial Killers and their Pets*.

"This is my staff," Dr. Quagmire gave a grand gesture acknowledging the people standing behind him, "These are your newest friends." Leaning down to Edgar, and whispering into his ear, "At your age, you're more likely to lose 15 friends in a day, that is if you *had* 15 friends. But here at the Relax Palace you just made 15 new friends just like that," Dr. Quagmire snapped his fingers.

"So Mr. Allen, welcome. We hope that your stay here will be a pleasant one." The staff members all applauded and some even called out, "Welcome home Edgar."

Edgar was silent. When the commotion died down he shouted, "I don't know what the hell is going on here, but I'm getting out of this loony bin." Edgar yanked the party hat from his head, threw it on the ground and began to get up from the bed. Suddenly, he found himself flanked by two mountains: Jerome and Frank. Jerome put a big thick hand on Edgar's left shoulder. Frank put his big beefy paw on Edgar's right shoulder, and they pushed him back into the bed. Pinned to the bed, and looking straight up, Edgar saw the face of Dr. Quagmire looking down on him. "Mr. Allen, we are not getting off to a very good start here. Let's start over, shall we? Your grandson, Gerry, called me to take you off his hands. Seems he was getting sick and tired of having to take care of Grandpappy all the time. That's why you're here. So, we can either play a little game called *Relax Palace* or *Pain Palace.* You choose Mr. Allen."

"You're nuts," shouted Edgar and he tried to wriggle free. "Let me go you stupid sons of bitches…I've done my time…"

"OK, have it your way Mr. Allen. Sedate him," screamed Dr. Quagmire. A nurse came running with a syringe. The doctor shoved the needle into Edgar's shoulder.

"I am going to fill you all with…you shit licking…sons of… bbbbb…." Edgar was out cold.

The Relax Palace

Edgar found the Relax Palace more depressing than prison. The hallways were filled with the near dead, all aimlessly shuffling their way to grave. It was a lifeless place, abnormally clean and filled with artificial sunlight. He couldn't stand it.

So, his stay at the Relax Palace was not what you would call a pleasant one.   He was unruly, hostile, angry, and had even tried to escape 3 times. As a result, he had spent a vast majority of his time at the Relax Palace in geriatric confinement. He was strapped into bed every night and was kept as groggy as possible so that they could better manage him during the day.   After several months of such treatment, he had become a defeated shell of a man.   When not strapped into bed, he would usually sit in a drug induced dullness in the TV room mindlessly repeating the phrase, "Boss man set me free."

One day Dr. Quagmire called Edgar into his office for a chat. Jerome and Frank carried him into the room.   They sat Edgar in a chair and stood behind him, their arms folded against their chests.

"Mr. Allen," Dr. Quagmire began, "you have been here at the Relax Palace for 3 months now, and it seems that you have been having a real problem acclimating yourself to our way of doing things."   While the doctor spoke Edgar was distracted and was busy taking in the office.   It was a luxurious office with a large mahogany desk and plush black leather chairs.   On the doctor's desk was a photo of Dr. Quagmire, with his wife and daughter, standing outside a house. Edgar assumed it was the doctor's house.

"Mr. Allen are you listening to me?" asked the doctor.

Edgar stared at the photo. His lips moved as if he were reading something.

"Mr. Allen," the doctor raised his voice. He then passed his hands in front of Edgar's face to see if he could capture his attention.

"Your family?" asked Edgar in a thin whisper.

"Yes," the doctor moved the photo out of Edgar's field of vision. "Can we have a chat Mr. Allen?"

"Yes."

"OK, good. So, as I was saying, you need to change the way you're behaving. You need to make an effort to fit in here at the Relax Palace. We can't keep pumping you full of drugs because it simply isn't cost effective. Drugs aren't cheap, Mr. Allen. So, here is what I propose. We draw a truce. You promise to change here and now and we can stop the drugs and the punishments. You can enjoy the same freedom as the other members of the Relax Palace. What do you say? Do you promise to be a good boy?"

Edgar nodded his head.

"Oh, excellent. So, it's a deal?"

"I've seen your house before… 2481 Parkwood?" whispered Edgar.

"No. 178 Elmwood…." the doctor, irritated that he was speaking to Edgar about his house, commanded Jerome and Frank, "OK, take him out of here."

As the men pulled Edgar out of his seat and dragged him from the office, Dr. Quagmire shouted, "You have two weeks Mr. Allen. Two weeks! If there is no change I just may have Jerome and Frank bury you alive." Jerome closed the office door and he and Frank dragged Edgar back to his room and strapped him into his bed.

A Changed Man

After that meeting Edgar was a changed man. He was pleasant with the staff. He was very cooperative. He even volunteered to help keep the community areas clean and tidy. He became a model citizen of the Relax Palace, and his crowning moment came when he was named *Relax Palace Resident of the Week*. The staff removed Mrs. Crandall's photo, who had been the *Resident of the Week* for the past 20 consecutive weeks. Mrs. Crandall didn't take her dethronement

16

well.   She cursed, spat and threw her morning juice at the staff members who were trying to take her photo off the wall.   As Mrs. Crandall was being strapped into her bed, Edgar's picture was hung in the TV room for everyone to see.

Slowly, he began to acquire the same privileges that the other community members enjoyed, and after two months of good behavior he was allowed to take his first constitutional. He was allowed to leave the premises of the Relax Palace on his own. The doctor was there to open the door for Edgar. He extended his hand to him and said, "Good show Mr. Allen."

Edgar beamed back to the doctor, "Thank you Dr. Quagmire." The two men shook hands. As Edgar walked down the stairs of the front entrance to the Relax Palace towards a waiting cab, the doctor said to himself, and to whomever was in the immediate proximity, "I am a certified miracle worker." Full of pride, the doctor smiled and waved to Edgar as he got into the cab.

Edgar P. Allen climbed into the backseat of the cab and commanded in a voice of broken glass, "178 Elmwood."   His destination, the Quagmire residence.

Edgar's Plan

The cab rolled to an ominous and quiet stop in front of the Quagmire house. Edgar sat in the backseat and peered out on the majestic homestead. He saw the perfectly pruned shrubs, the neatly manicured lawn and the blue sky filled with fluffy white clouds. It was a place that Edgar believed was disinfected from pain. He grinned to himself as he thought about the suffering that he wished to bring to the Quagmires.

The day that Edgar had seen the photo of Dr. Quagmire

17

standing in front of his enormous white house, pompously grinning, his arm around his wife's shoulders, his other arm around his daughter, Edgar had the uncontrollable urge to destroy the squeaky clean suburban happiness that lived in the photo.

So, from that day forward, Edgar tried hard to befriend his enemy in order to learn his weakness. As the time passed, Edgar discovered that the doctor was a remarkably stingy man that treasured his daughter.

Edgar envisioned this as his last battle, and the stakes were high. He was going to fight the doctor for redemption from a life lived in a cage. Dr. Quagmire became The Oppressor - the living symbol of all the forces that had destroyed Edgar's life.

Edgar barked at the cab driver, "159 Mocking Bird Way."

Shem

Edgar knew that he couldn't do this job alone. He would only be able to leave the Relax Palace for a couple hours a day, and he needed someone to watch the Quagmires for him, someone that he could trust.

Edgar didn't have many choices. He had only one friend; a man he had met in prison - a strange and enigmatic man called Shem. Edgar liked to think of Shem as a freak of nature, like a storm that rains blood. Almost everyone that had ever met Shem agreed that he was a mystery for the simple reason that he was incommunicable. Being both illiterate and mute, the only means of communication left for Shem was a series of ambiguous hand signs and body gestures, or guttural grunts and groans.

One night, a long time ago, as Edgar and Shem sat in their prison cell, Shem had tried to, at least Edgar believed Shem was trying

18

to, explain the reason he was in jail. All Edgar was able to decipher, from the kinetic symphony of inarticulate hand gestures accompanied by raspy croaks and cawing, was that Shem was beyond comprehension.

Edgar drove out in the cab to 159 Mocking Bird Way in order to tell his friend his assignment: he was to videotape the Quagmire house night and day so that Edgar could determine how and when they would strike.

And thus the time passed...

As the months passed and as Edgar studied tape after tape searching for a rhythm, a pattern, in the absences of Dr. and Mrs. Quagmire, he began to have doubts about this criminal endeavor he was planning. He began to think that he was merely wasting his and Shem's time. He even began to convince himself that the whole idea of one last crime, a crime against the repugnant Dr. Quagmire, was merely his way to stop thinking about death. It was merely a preoccupation - nothing else. Edgar began to feel particularly despondent when he realized that he and Shem would never be able to pull off the kidnapping, not alone at least. They were too old, too weak, too blind, too fragile, too slow. They would need help. They would need to recruit a third person, someone preferably younger than Shem or himself. Someone who could help with the grunt work. But who?

Jonah Dickson

Jonah Dickson was an exceptional thief. Although he was only 17 years old, he had put together a resume of burglaries, cons, cheats, thefts, and swindles that would put the most ambitious, hardest working thieves to shame. But Jonah had one small problem: bad luck.

Not only did he never manage to steal anything of value, it seemed that unkind Fate had doomed him to failure, for in fact, anything that could go wrong on a Jonah Dickson burglary always did.

Jonah's first foray into the life of crime came at the young and vulnerable age of 13. When most boys his age were studying algebra, playing video games, and chasing girls, Jonah was planning his first theft: a pickup truck at the local White Whale gas station. Laying on his belly in a patch of dandelions in a vacant lot across the street from the gas station, Jonah watched through a pair of binoculars as the owner of the pickup started pumping gas and then sauntered into the station office. Jonah saw the keys glisten in the sunlight as they dangled from the ignition.

This was the moment he had been waiting for all morning long. He dashed across the road, sidled up to the driver side of the pickup, slid into the cab and started the truck. He stomped the gas pedal to the floor. The tires spun wildly, and smoke billowed outside the vehicle like it was a rocket launching into space. The pickup burst out of the gas station with the gas pump nozzle still firmly anchored into truck's gas tank; the hose ripped free from the pump and gas spurted everywhere. Out of control, the truck careened into the median in the middle of the road. Jonah frantically turned the steering wheel, pointed the truck in the right direction and was gone.

He saw the truck's owner in the rear view mirror chasing after him. But soon the owner and the gas station were far out of sight, and Jonah began to relax. He turned up the radio. **Confusion Reactor's** *Glass Digits/Emergency Launch*, a wild jungle-beat spaceship romp piloted by Elmore James past the moons of Jupiter, put a smile on his face. He sat back deep in the seat, rolled down the window and felt the fresh air in his face. He was exhilarated. He became giddy when he thought about pulling the truck up to his home. Oh, how proud his somewhat drunken swindler of a father would be.

But Jonah learned a valuable lesson that day. Gas stations are not ideal places for stealing cars. He was able to travel two miles before the truck sputtered to a stop. Crushed by the fact that the vehicle was out of gas, he pulled over to the shoulder of the road, parked the truck and walked dejectedly home.

Perhaps, though, Jonah's most legendary caper was the time he attempted to burgle the Vanderbrocks. The Vanderbrocks were a wealthy couple, and as such, they had lavish tastes. Mrs. Vanderbrock owned a fine collection of jewelry that had merited an article in the local newspaper. She was quoted as saying, "And this necklace cost my husband, George, $5,000." That was all Jonah needed to read.

So, Jonah surveyed the Vanderbrock house. He kept meticulous notes of the comings and goings of the Vanderbrocks, and after three weeks of surveillance he had enough data to recognize a trend. Mr. Vanderbrock would leave for work every morning between the hours of 8:45 and 9:15, and every Wednesday Mrs. Vanderbrock would leave at 11:00 and would return home at 4:30 in the afternoon. So, Wednesday it was.

That Wednesday everything went like clockwork. Mr. Vanderbrock kissed his wife goodbye at 8:55, and Mrs. Vanderbrock made her exit at precisely 11:00. Jonah easily picked the lock of the front door. Now all he had to do was find the jewelry.

He knew he had ample time and was in no great hurry. Jonah casually explored the living room, inspecting the CD's that Vanderbrocks owned. Dissatisfied with their rather skimpy collection of completely generic and flavorless music, he wandered into the kitchen where he perused their pantries and refrigerator, helping himself to a beer. Eventually, he meandered up the stairs to their bedroom. This is where Jonah's instincts told him he would find the goods.

He was looking through their dresser drawers when he heard voices. He froze. The front door opened. Jonah didn't know where to hide. He ran to the closet. It was filled with boxes; he couldn't fit inside. He heard footsteps and laughter coming from the stairs. He fell to the ground and slid underneath the bed. Suddenly, the bedroom door burst open and Mrs. Vanderbrock and some man Jonah had never seen before tumbled into the room and onto the bed. They groped and they grappled. They moaned and maneuvered, and before long the bed was bouncing like a trampoline.

Jonah had no choice but to wait out the lust that was brewing above. He laid on his stomach under the bed irritated by this unexpected intrusion, cursing his bad luck. But after a solid 15 minutes of Mrs. Vanderbrock screaming in ecstasy, he forgot all about his bad luck. He decided he had to take a peak. He quietly pulled himself out from under the bed and slowly raised his head to take a look at the intertwined couple.

At first you could describe Jonah's gazing as casual observance, but after 5 minutes of repositioning himself to get a better look at this or that he could officially be called a *voyeur*. Jonah stationed himself at the foot of the bed, and he watched the couple, on hands and knees, through the brass floral pattern of the bed's footboard.

Suddenly, the bedroom door burst open for the second time. This time it was Mr.Vanderbrock. With eyes full of rage and his hunting rifle in his hand, he surveyed the room. His gaze traveled from the bed to Jonah, then back to the bed and then back to Jonah. He

22

didn't quite know what to make of the situation. His expression was that of a question mark. Finally he spoke, "What kind of sick perverted...." Words, though, began to fail him and Mr. Vanderbrock thought that he could express himself more succinctly with the rifle.

Mrs. Vanderbrock had hid herself from her husband behind a pillow. She peeked over the top of the pillow in order to assess just how angry her husband was, and she spotted Jonah on his knees at the footboard. Disgusted by the thought of someone breaking into a house to spy on two people having sex, she pointed an accusing finger at Jonah and said, "Sweetheart, I have no idea who that strange and obviously perverted boy is or how he got in here. Shoot him dead!"

So, Mr. Vanderbrock aimed at Jonah. But seeing his naked wife in the arms of another man was a good enough argument to change his mind regarding who should be "shot dead." So he pointed the gun at the man in the bed.

"Oh, for the love of god," pleaded the man, clinging to Mrs. Vanderbrock like a drowning man clinging to a life preserver, "please don't shoot me!"

Mr. Vanderbrock advanced toward the bed and spat venomously, "And why shouldn't I shoot you? Here you are, screwing *my* wife in *my* bed. You dirty..."

Jonah took this as his cue to make his exit. While Mr. Vanderbrock was preoccupied with Mrs. Vanderbrock's lover, he ran and jumped through the bedroom window and plummeted to the ground. He landed with a thud in the front yard. He quickly pulled himself up with the intention of breaking into a mad dash to save his life, but his body didn't cooperate. He was forced to limp away. As he lamely staggered from the house, he could hear gunshots and the voices of Mrs. Vanderbrock and her lover screaming in chorus, "Shoot him! He's getting away." Such was the luck of Jonah Dickson.

The Greasy Burger

Since he was unable to support himself as a thief, Jonah Dickson had to live like a *straight*. And so it was that he found a job at the Greasy Burger diner as a short order cook. Jonah detested the job. He especially disliked the customers. The diner was usually frequented by drunks and cheapskates. No matter who the customer was though, they always complained about the food. "This is overcooked…how do expect me to eat this without Mayo…I asked for rare not raw…This isn't fit for my dog…" Every day there was a new litany of complaints.

As if the customers weren't bad enough, Jonah abhorred the owner of the Greasy Burger, a man that everyone knew as Wheezy. Wheezy was a grotesquely obese man. He weighed close to half a ton and was called *Wheezy* because any sort of action, such as standing up, would cause Wheezy to begin wheezing like a marathon runner at the end of a race. Wheezy, though, could have easily been given the name *Stinky*, because anyone within a 3 foot radius of him was bound to get a whiff of a stench so foul and rotten that it would automatically trigger the gag reflex. Jonah imagined that being so large must make bathing, among other things, rather difficult.

Wheezy was generally disliked because of his freakish girth and his odor. Even his own mother was unable to love him. Sometimes she would show up at the diner to berate her son. They would end up screaming at one another, but in the end Wheezy's mother always got what she came for: money. Wheezy, like a well trained dog, would open the cash register and pull out a couple fives, a ten maybe, never anymore, and hand them to her in a gesture of

24

reconciliation for yelling at her. She would take the money and again berate him. Jonah enjoyed the days when Wheezy's mother would make an appearance at the diner.

To make matters worst, also plaguing Jonah was the fact that he came from a long line of cheats and swindles and he could feel the pressure of his pedigree. Every morning that he tied the grease stained apron around his waist was a painful reminder that he was a disappointment to his forefathers. What would his father say if he saw him working? He never worked a day in his life. Jonah began to think of himself as a failure. He was filled with self-doubt and he began to believe his life was a disaster.

But as luck would have it, one auspicious summer day, salvation arrived at the Greasy Burger in the form of Edgar P. Allen. Jonah was sitting at a counter near the grill reading a newspaper. Wheezy was manning the cash register as usual, when none other than Edgar P. Allen walked into the Greasy Burger. Edgar sat in a booth near a window and barked out to Jonah, "Are you going to wait on me today or should I come back tomorrow?"

Jonah slowly, languidly strolled over to the booth. He stood there for a moment taking in the old man. Edgar was a thin, wiry man. His face was dull, the expression of which had been worn down with age until it only expressed the ghost of who he once was. He sat at the booth with a scowling, lethal bitterness.

"What do you want?" asked Jonah expressionlessly.

Edgar complained, "Coffee, black and scrambled eggs."

"You want toast with that?"

"If I wanted toast I would have asked for it, goddamn it," spat Edgar.

Jonah gave Edgar one last look and then turned to go back to the grill.

"And make it snappy, kid. I don't got all day," said Edgar. Jonah stopped in his tracks and cringed. He wanted to retaliate, to say something, but he thought better of it and silently went back to the grill to prepare the food. On his way to the grill he had to pass Wheezy. About 10 or 15 flies were in orbit around him.

So, there was Jonah, standing over the grill scrambling eggs, filled with existential angst and impotent rage when Edgar again shouted, "Hey kid, I changed my mind. Make those eggs over easy."

Wheezy, bracing himself at the cash register, decided he needed to explain the Greasy Burger policy regarding mistake orders. "Jonah, I hope you understand that I will have to deduct those eggs from your pay. Whenever you make a mistake like that, make something that the customer doesn't want, you will have to pay for it. OK?"

Jonah turned to Wheezy, "What the hell are you talking about? That old fart ordered scrambled eggs. I didn't make any mistake."

"Who are you calling an old fart, you little prick," yelled Edgar springing to his feet.

"Please sir, sit down. Your eggs will be ready in a moment," urged Wheezy.

Suddenly, without warning, Jonah Dickson did something of which he had never dreamed he was capable. He grabbed a knife from the counter walked to where Wheezy was standing, encountered the stench barrier that protected Wheezy from predators, froze momentarily, took a deep breath and proceeded. Wheezy, who was using the cash register as a crutch to hold up his massive frame, his back to Jonah, was unaware that Jonah was behind him until he felt a sharp object against the back of his neck. "Open the cash register or I swear I'll cut your fat head off," demanded Jonah through clenched teeth, holding his breath. Wheezy stood motionless.

"Open it," screamed Jonah as he pressed the knife hard against the back of Wheezy's neck. Jonah heard the register open and he strained to look past Wheezy to see what the register contained but the massive mound of man blocked his view.

"OK, hand me the money," Jonah shouted.

"But there isn't much here" reasoned Wheezy. "We just opened, Jonah. We have a couple fives, some ones…"

"Don't talk," Jonah howled, "just give me the money." He was trying desperately to hold his breath.

"Do you want the dimes and nickels too?"

"I don't want the change," said Jonah as he pulled away from Wheezy with a fistful of ten one dollar bills and a single five.

Jonah turned to Edgar, "You."

"Me?"

"Yes, you…you old fart. Stand up. I'm taking you hostage."

"Hostage?"said Edgar unable to believe what he was hearing.

"Shut up and get moving." Jonah went up to Edgar with the knife. He grabbed the old man and started to push him from behind towards the door, holding the knife to his back.

Jonah's car was parked on the street outside the diner - a blue Dodge Eris 5 door. Jonah pushed Edgar in the direction of his Dodge Eris and forced him into the passenger seat. He raced around to the other side of the car. As he sat down in the driver seat, he saw that Wheezy had begun the laborious 15 foot journey from the cash register to the telephone. Wheezy was already huffing and puffing like a locomotive after traveling only a couple of feet. Although Jonah had plenty of time to make his getaway, he still found himself instinctively in a frenzied hurry. So, he rushed nervously, and as he did so he began to create problems where problems didn't exist. At first he couldn't find his car keys. He pulled everything out of his pants pockets in a panic. After finding the keys, he had trouble inserting the key into the ignition.   Once he eventually managed to shove the key into the ignition, he turned it and the car coughed then moaned and slowly belched into life. Jonah pointed the knife at Edgar and said, "Don't try anything funny," as the car jerked and sputtered away from the Greasy Burger.

Jonah's Hostage

"So what's the plan now kid? You want to sell me back to my family?" Edgar was foaming with rage. "Well they don't want me!" He screamed so loudly that it actually frightened Jonah causing the car to swerve.

"Shut up," Jonah snapped back at Edgar. The truth was that Jonah didn't know what to do. The only idea he had was to pull the car over and run away. But he was determined he was going to make this work. He was going to get something from this old man. Failure was not an option.

"You have a bank account?" Jonah asked.

"No." replied Edgar.

"Give me your wallet," Jonah demanded.

"Sure, hold on a second." Edgar reached into his pocket, and the next thing Jonah knew, Edgar was pointing a gun at him.

Surprised by the state of affairs and how this spontaneous robbery/hostage taking was going from bad to worse. Jonah protested, "You have a gun? You....but you must be 90 years old? What's this world coming to?"

"Make a right at the next light," Edgar barked.

Jonah did as he was told. They drove for a bit until they came to the edge of town. Edgar had Jonah turn off the main road onto a small dirt road. The road cut through a field of wild grass and weeds turned yellow by the summer sun. At the end of the road was a small dilapidated shack. Jonah stopped the car.

Jonah saw the miserable little shack as a fitting end to his life. He was to be killed by this ancient man sitting next to him and his body would be left here at this rotting, collapsing shack. "Go ahead, shoot me. Come on, take me out of my misery," said Jonah.

Edgar tossed the gun on the dashboard and rolled his window down. "Kid, you don't know misery," Edgar growled.

Edgar had been sitting in the passenger seat ruminating over the fact that he had been taken hostage. But as the two drove he began to calm down and he began to realize something: this boy just might be useful.

There was a long awkward silence as the two men sat in the car in the hot sunlight.

Edgar's frown loosened a bit, and he spoke with what could be described as agitated tenderness. "Listen kid, I think you're bit," trying to be diplomatic, Edgar was searching for the right word rather than blurting out the first thing that came to his mind, "I think you're a bit confused. First of all, you only take a hostage in a situation where you are trying to bargain for something. You've seen those bank robber movies, right? Secondly, you should have taken the money from the register. That fat bastard had more than the 25 bucks he gave you. And what about his wallet? Why didn't you take his wallet?"

But Jonah just sat there, dejected by the whole "robbery / hostage taking" that had earned him a total of $15. He began to talk to

29

no one in particular, "All I want is for one time things to go right. One time. Just to steal something once without screwing everything up."

Edgar gave Jonah a careful, curious glance. This kid is going down in flames, he thought. Edgar was not interested in a playing the part of the philanthropist, but he began to think that maybe this boy could help him, and who knows, thought Edgar, maybe, just maybe, the kid will be better off too. Finally, Edgar asked, "Would you be interested in a business proposition?"

The Business Proposition

Edgar invited Jonah inside the shack to talk things over. Jonah was surprised to find that it was rather neat and tidy inside. He had thought, based on the outside appearance of the shack, that it would be a dusty, cobwebbed room filled with ominous shadows and murky darkness; instead, there was one large living area with a small dining table, a counter with a gas stovetop, a small bathroom with a toilet and a sink, and across from the door where the Jonah and Edgar entered, there was another door which was closed. Jonah assumed that was the bedroom.

"You live here?" asked Jonah.

"No," said Edgar. "An old friend of mine has been staying here," he added with a wicked smile.

The two men sat down at the table and Edgar said, as he fidgeted in his seat, "Getting older is like...well...you know it's like a time bomb going off. Everything seems to go at once. The teeth, I don't even want to talk about the dentist, and then there are the cataracts. Christ, I can barely..." Edgar couldn't believe that he was confessing his aches and pains to this strange kid. Irritated with himself, he quickly changed the tone of his monologue and continued,

"I know this son of a bitch that needs to feel what it's like to be vulnerable. He needs to feel a little pain. You know what I mean? Getting older isn't a crime. I've done my time. I'm a free man..." Edgar was becoming vehement and was banging his withered fists on the table. He stopped and composed himself and began again, "Anyway, one day I got to thinking, what would hurt him the most? Well, I did a little snooping around and I found that this bastard adores two things in life: his daughter and his ducats."

"Ducats?" puzzled Jonah.

"Money," snapped Edgar.

Edgar pulled a box down from a shelf and he pulled out a few photos, three or four, and flipped through them. He then strained to read something on the back of one of the photos. Satisfied, he handed the photo to Jonah.

"That's her. Angie Quagmire. She isn't much to look at...a bit on the hefty side...but her old man adores her. Why? The hell if I know. I only know that if she went missing he would be devastated. And once he sees the amount of the ransom he'll have a heart attack. "

"How old is she?" asked Jonah.

"18 or 19. I'm not really sure."

"So, you want to steal this Angie Quagmire girl?"

"Most people call it *kidnapping*," scowled Edgar.

The Details of the Plan

Edgar didn't want Jonah to know that he resided in an old age home. So, he had Jonah drive him to the bus stop not too far from the Relax Palace. Edgar would pretend to be waiting for a bus, and once Jonah would drive off he would return to the Relax Palace.

As Jonah drove, Edgar explained, "I've got everything worked out. I've been watching the Quagmires for a couple months now, and every other Tuesday they go to a friend's house for some drinks and poker. They don't get back until late. It's a sure thing. We just show up on Tuesday and nab the girl."

Jonah was preoccupied with one thing only: money. "How much will the ransom be?" He could have cared less about the details of the kidnapping.

"$500,000," Edgar said slowly and seductively, watching Jonah carefully.

"Not bad," said Jonah trying his hardest not to let his poker face slip, but Edgar was able to detect the faint outline of a smile on the young man's face.

The math was easy, $250,000 each. The day began with a botched robbery / hostage taking that had earned him a lousy $15 and was ending with the prospect of the nearly unimaginable $250,000.

"Leave me off here," said Edgar as they approached the bus stop near the Relax Palace. Jonah pulled the car to the side of the road. As Edgar opened the door to get out, he added, "We split it three ways."

"There's someone else?" asked Jonah disappointed that his share of the money had gone from $250,000 to $166,666.66 in a matter of seconds.

"An old friend," Edgar smiled viciously.

The Deep South, the Hot Lands

On the day the kidnapping was to take place, Edgar had asked Jonah to meet him at the shack at the end of the dirt road at 9:30 in the evening so that they could drive out to his grandson's office and steal a delivery van. "I have a grandson, believe it or not, and he, like a good law abiding citizen, has started a business. He runs a courier service. Well, we're going to steal one of his delivery vans," Edgar had explained to Jonah.

When Jonah arrived at the shack he found Edgar sitting with another old man. "Jonah this is Shem," Edgar said. Shem didn't look nearly as old as Edgar, but he did look as though he had been dead for a couple of days. There was something about him that made Jonah immediately think of decay. Shem was skeleton thin, his skin was the color of cigarette ash and he stank of mothballs. His eyes were hazy and gray, and Jonah wondered if the old man could see at all. Shem extended a scrawny crows foot of a hand and Jonah shook it reluctantly. Jonah was puzzled. He didn't quite understand what role Shem could play in this kidnapping.

"Shem is from the *nether lands* if you know what I mean," said Edgar with a hollow smile.

"Holland?"

"No," complained Edgar, "the deep south. The hot lands."

"Oh," said Jonah feigning that he understood what Edgar was talking about.

Stealing the Van

"I don't know why we have to steal a car. We can just use mine," said Jonah as he and Edgar drove out to Allen's Courier Service.

"This piece of crap? Anyway, we're supposed to be delivery men," grunted Edgar.

When they arrived at Allen's Courier Service, Jonah parked his car across the street from the building. Jonah and Edgar sat studying the dark and quiet lot of vehicles that belonged to Gerry Allen.

Edgar hadn't committed a crime in a long, long time, and being so close to actually stealing something made his heart race and his hands shake. "Once, when I was a kid I stole a priest from a church," snapped Edgar excitedly.

"You mean you *kidnapped* a priest," corrected Jonah.

"No," glowered Edgar. "I stole him. There was no ransom...it was a bar bet. Now you made me lose my train of thought," he frowned. "Never mind."

"Well, I've never hotwired a car before," Jonah admitted.

"Don't worry, kid. My idiot grandson has a key to the front door hidden under the welcome mat. There won't be any need to hotwire anything."

Jonah and Edgar sat silently, both of them staring at the office. As Jonah waited for Edgar to give the word, he daydreamed about sitting in a lavish restaurant, drinking champagne and eating lobster. His daydream also came furnished with a beautiful blond woman, scantily dressed, clinging to his arm. He daydreamed of the good life. A life with money. But Jonah's meditations were cut short. Edgar pushed open the passenger door and barked, "Let's go."

Jonah raced quickly to the front door of the office, while Edgar strolled slowly behind him. When Edgar finally arrived at the front door, Jonah whispered angrily, "What are you doing? Do you want someone to see us?"

Edgar replied at full volume, "Who's going to see us?"

Suddenly, a ring of light illuminated Edgar's face.

Edgar and Jonah turned in the direction of the light. Standing a couple of feet from them was a security guard pointing a flashlight at them.

"What do you two think you're doing?" the guard asked.

Edgar shielded the light from his eyes with his hands and squinted in the direction of the security guard, "Would you get that thing out of my eyes," he demanded.

Jonah was stunned silent by the presence of the security guard and was contemplating ditching the old man and running for the car. But Edgar felt great. He felt just like he did when he was a young man in his prime. He took a few moments and studied the security guard. He was young, with a fuzzy upper lip, a face flattened by stupidity, and enormous, fleshy ears, like two hands attached to the sides of his head.

"We are investigative reporters," said Edgar. "We are investigating the level of security of the shops in this area." Edgar smiled a withered smile and continued, "We are trying to see how difficult it would be to steal something from one of these shops."

"Well, it would be pretty difficult to steal something from Allen's Courier Service, because I'm here," said the guard as he turned off the flashlight.

"You're right. But, unfortunately, *that* won't sell any newspapers."

"What do you mean?" asked the guard, scratching his head with the butt end of the flashlight.

"Well, no one wants to read a story about people being safe. We want stories with danger, with violence," said Edgar as he wadded his right hand into an excited fist.

The guard continued to scratch his head.

"So how about this, we write a story about this business, Allen's Courier Service being robbed? What do you think? You could even be the hero of the story," Edgar leaned toward the guard and winked knowingly at him.

The guard stopped scratching his head and just stared dully at

35

Edgar. If you were to look deep into his eyes you would have been able to see the cogs churning, thoughts were being manufactured inside his rather vacuous head.

"What's your name?" asked Edgar.

"Davey," said the guard.

"Take that down kid," spat Edgar over his shoulder to Jonah.

Jonah, still a bit uncertain of the situation, said quietly, "But I don't have a pen."

"You can use mine," said Davey pulling a pen from his shirt pocket and offering it to Jonah.

Jonah wasn't exceptionally excited. "I don't have any paper."

"Make a mental note for Christ's sake. His name is Davey. It's not that difficult to remember," spat Edgar impatiently.

Then Edgar told Davey, "So here is the story as I see it, a couple of drug crazed lunatics, looking to steal a delivery van, show up. They threaten you at gunpoint and demand the keys to the office."

"But I don't have any keys," replied Davey.

"You don't have any keys but they don't believe you, and threaten to blow your head off. Then, you remember that there is a spare key underneath the welcome mat." Edgar lifted the mat and there, shining in the moonlight, was a single silver key.

"Wow," exclaimed Davey. "How did you do that?" He obviously thought that Edgar was some sort of magician and that he had made the key materialize out of thin air.

"They go inside the office, find keys for a van and steal one. You of course, being a brave guy, jump in front of the van..."

"Yeah. I jump in front of the van and it swerves to keep from running me over. Then I grab onto the side mirror. They drive off with me holding on..." Davey was infected with the spirit of storytelling.

36

"Are you getting all this?" Edgar asked Jonah.

Jonah remained silent.

"...and then I swing into the truck and we start fighting..."

"You have a future in journalism kid," said Edgar with a crooked smile. "So, in order to make sure that the story can be corroborated, I suggest that my partner and I take a van for a couple of hours..."

"In case another reporter stops by? Maybe a reporter investigating investigative reporters?" said Davey earnestly.

"Absolutely." Edgar was stunned by what he was hearing. He reasoned that the average person's level of common sense had taken a sharp nose dive while he was in prison. Stealing something was never this easy when Edgar was growing up.

The Kidnapping

When Jonah and Edgar returned to the shack, they found Shem where they had left him, except he was wearing a blue jumpsuit and a blue baseball cap.

Edgar went into the shack and came out with two more jumpsuits and caps, one for him and one for Jonah. Jonah struggled with his. The suit that he was given was for a midget. He fought his way into it. He looked down and saw that the pant legs ended at the middle of his shins. The sleeves ended at his forearms, and in general the suit was painfully tight.

"Edgar, maybe I could trade suits with you or Shem. This one doesn't fit too well." Edgar came over and examined the suit. "Yeah it's a bit small...but it'll do."

Jonah looked down and saw that a patch bearing a name had been sewn onto the left breast pocket of his suit. The name read

Mabel.

"It says here that my name is *Mabel.*"

Edgar again scrutinized the suit, "So it does. We'll have to put a piece of masking tape over the name."

"Maybe I should just wait in the car?"

Edgar ignored Jonah. "OK, let's make sure we have everything," he announced. "Ransom note?" Shem pulled out an envelope containing the letter from his left breast pocket. "Clipboard with pen?" Shem held up a clipboard and a pen. "Do we need anything else?" Shem shook his head "no."

"What about chloroform or something like that to knock out the girl?" asked Jonah, a bit confused by the sparse inventory of items.

"Don't worry about that. Shem will take care of that," replied Edgar gruffly.

"But I don't..." Jonah was cut short by Edgar who scowled at him. He considered it wise to keep any other questions to himself.

With nothing left to say, Jonah climbed into the driver seat of the van. As Jonah sat behind the wheel, he had the uncanny feeling that his father's spirit was whisking about on that moonlit night. He even imagined that he could hear his father's voice in the breeze, and it said, "I knew you could do it son." Unfortunately, Jonah's spirits began to dwindle as he watched Edgar and Shem hobble slowly to the van. Jonah even began to entertain doubt: maybe this wasn't such a good idea. As Edgar pulled himself into the passenger seat wincing and panting, Jonah's thoughts took on a much darker tone. We'll be lucky if we don't get arrested before the night is over.

As Shem climbed into the van, Edgar said, trying to catch his breath, "Let's get a move on."

The Quagmire house was located in the Back Woods suburb,

a suburb of enormous houses that were usually occupied by young childless couples that were desperately devoted to their jobs, SUV's, cell phones and any and all digital appliances. Each house was a replica of the previous and all nature that surrounded the houses, such as bushes or shrubs, was pruned and trimmed with such geometric precision that it was impossible to believe it was not invented by man.

When the men reached the Quagmire house they saw that Dr. Quagmire's car was still in the driveway, so they drove around the block and parked a couple of houses down from the Quagmire place.

Edgar looked at his watch "10:30," he said, "The good doctor and his wife should be stepping out soon."

So they waited, and as they waited Jonah could feel his stomach twisting and turning: nerves. His bowels clenched and he started squirming in his seat in order to quell the discomfort.

Edgar peered over at Jonah and asked, "Are you going to be OK?" Jonah nodded.

And so the men waited.

Shortly after 10:40 the Quagmires left the house, got in the doctor's car and drove away.

"We'll wait a little bit longer," Edgar informed Jonah and Shem. "Just to be sure."

Jonah began to feel the need to use the toilet. He began fluttering his legs from side to side, and he clenched his gut desperately trying to hold back the threat of the imminent explosion. Edgar, seeing the state Jonah was in, decided that if they waited any longer Jonah ran the chance of fouling himself. That would spoil everything. He ordered Jonah to pull into the driveway. The three kidnappers got out of the vehicle and walked to the front door. Jonah was hunched over holding his stomach.

"Stand up straight," Edgar growled.

At 10:43 Edgar rang the doorbell of the Quagmire residence.

"I think I should just wait in the..." Before Jonah could finish his statement the door opened. It was still chain bolted from the inside, but Angie Quagmire stared at the three strangers standing on her porch through the opening. The men could only see one of her brown eyes, her nose and portion of her mouth.

"Sorry to disturb you so late Miss, but we have a special delivery letter for Mr...Dr. Quagmire," said Edgar.

"Isn't it a bit late to be delivering letters?" asked Angie incredulously.

"Oooohhhhh," groaned Jonah.

Edgar gave Jonah a kick in the shin and continued loudly in order to drown out Jonah's moaning, "Yes it is Miss. But it seems that there was a mix up at the office and this letter was overlooked somehow. It was supposed to have been delivered this morning."

Through the opening, Angie looked from one man to the next. Finally she asked, "Is he OK?" referring to Jonah.

"He's fine. He's got a bit of indigestion though," Edgar felt proud for such quick thinking.

As Angie peered at the men through the opening, Edgar detected that she was not buying the charade. So he decided to bluff, "If you want we can leave a receipt and the doctor can come down and pick up the letter himself tomorrow morning."

Angie folded, "No, that's OK." She knew her father detested waiting in line for anything. So, she closed the door, unlocked the chain bolt, and reopened the door. Angie Quagmire stood framed by the doorway. She was wearing a cream colored nightgown covered with miniature suns and shooting stars, and all around her the light from the hallway spilled over her and shone as if it were a corona. Jonah took in this vision, this young woman and his mouth fell open. She's an angel, he thought.

"What's wrong with him now?" Angie asked pointing to Jonah.

Edgar turned to Jonah, and gave him a dirty look. Jonah registered the dirty look from Edgar and shook himself free from the trance and closed his mouth.

"Sorry Miss. He's a bit *slow*, if you know what I mean" whispered Edgar to Angie.

Angie craned her neck in order to look past Edgar and get a better glimpse of Jonah. "His name is Mabel?"

"Oh, no. That isn't his uniform. It belongs to his mother," Edgar improvised.

Jonah began to tug at the sleeve of Edgar's uniform. Edgar slapped at Jonah's hand, but Jonah persisted. Finally, an irritated Edgar turned and asked, "What is it?"

Jonah leaned towards Edgar and whispered, "That's not the girl....she's not the one in the picture you showed me."

"Did he say something about a picture?" inquired the young Angie.

"He...he...thinks he saw you in a magazine or something..." Edgar was doing his best.

"So, if you would just sign here we can be on our way," Edgar handed the girl the clipboard and Shem handed her the pen.

She took both of them reluctantly, and as she was about to sign she stopped and asked, "Aren't you a bit old to be working?"

Edgar found the question offensive. He responded with great restraint and with the best fake smile that he could muster, "I am actually retiring tonight. This is my last delivery."

Angie was finding all of this very strange but, anyway, she took the pen and put it to paper and again stopped, "Why are there three of you? That's not very cost effective?"

Cost effective? The words hit Edgar like a punch to the face. She is her old man's daughter, he thought. "Listen kid, we're just trying to deliver a package. We didn't know that we were going to be interrogated by the Gestapo," he snapped.

She signed the form, Edgar collected the clipboard and Shem snatched the pen. Shem then handed her the envelope containing the ransom note. The men bid Angie good night and Angie silently slipped back inside and closed the door behind her.

Shem, holding the pen, closed his eyes. He began to chant something. It was at this moment that Jonah thought he understood what Edgar was trying to tell him about Shem. "Is he a witch doctor or something?" Jonah asked Edgar.

"Keep your mouth shut," hissed Edgar as he put his ear to the door.

Suddenly the door snapped open, and Angie stood before the men, "What the hell is going on out here? What does he think he's doing?" referring to Shem.

"I think he's having a seizure," said Edgar innocently.

"This has gone far enough. If this is some sort of warped reality TV show, then you better stop..." Angie began to swoon. Shem's incantations became louder.

"Get ready to catch her when she falls," Edgar yelled to Jonah.

Jonah stepped into the hallway and standing behind Angie the two danced a drunken dance as Angie swooned and swayed under the influence of Shem, and then it was done. She collapsed into Jonah's arms. He laid her on the floor and looked at her. He then looked up at Shem and said, "That was amazing." Shem smiled a deceased smile.

"She...she's...beautiful," Jonah stammered to Edgar. "She isn't the girl you showed me in the photo. This isn't her. She....she..."

"Listen prince charming, don't get any funny ideas. Just load her into the van."

The Wrong Girl?

When the kidnappers returned to the shack at the end of the dirt road, Edgar was tired of hearing Jonah insistently ask, "Are you sure this is the right girl?" No matter how loudly or how politely Edgar would scream that this girl in the delivery van was in fact, he was 100% certain of it, Angie Quagmire, Jonah would persist, "But this isn't the girl in the picture you showed me." Jonah reasoned aloud, "Maybe she was having a sleepover? Maybe one of the girls sleeping over answered the door? Did you ever think of that?" Edgar sat silently staring out the window. He couldn't believe the stupidity of the suggestion. But, nonetheless, he began to mull over the statistical probability of a sleepover. Edgar had always found statistics dull and he began contemplating more concrete matters like, girls painting each other's toenails, girls in pink panties jumping up and down on Angie's bed, girls taking showers together; he stopped himself there.

So when the men entered the shack, Edgar marched to the box containing his personal items. Jonah stood behind him. "Quit breathing down my neck," Edgar hissed turning away from Jonah.

He pulled out the photos, and as he flipped through them Jonah announced, "There. That was the one you showed me." Edgar squinted and strained to make sense of the figure in the photo. Staring

Edgar in the face was a picture of his dead wife. She was probably 28 or 29 in the photo. Her name was Violet. Edgar's blood boiled. He stared at that picture with a nuclear hostility. "Even from the grave…" he started to stammer. "…even from the grave you have to ruin everything." He tore the picture in half and then tore both halves in half and threw the pieces on the floor.

Shem was standing in the doorway silent and impassive. "What are you staring at?" shouted Edgar. Then he barked at Jonah, "And you, what are you standing there for? Bring the girl into the house!"

Jonah ran to the van for Angie. He was not able to pick her up since he wasn't exceptionally strong, and so he dragged her from the van into the house. He pulled her by her armpits and placed her in the room that he had conjectured was a bedroom.

The dilapidated shack's bedroom was a dismal, windowless room that smelled of mildew. In one corner of the room, lit up by the light that flowed in from the open door, was a bed. The rest of the room, though, was a eerie mystery shrouded in darkness.

Edgar handed Jonah some rope and Jonah quickly tied the girl's hands and feet.

"So, who's the girl in the photo, then?" asked Jonah timidly as he tied.

"Shut up," snapped Edgar. "We've got the right girl. I showed you the wrong picture." Edgar muttered more to himself than anyone else. Turning to Shem he said, "Sorry, old pal. Now, wake her up."

Anal Deficiency

Dr. Quagmire and his wife, Dorothy, returned home at about 1:30 in the morning. Dr. Quagmire had had a miserable time as usual.

He disliked one of the guests at the party, a man named Steve Mitchell. Mitchell was the doctor's omnipresent neighbor; he spent a suspicious amount of time at the doctor's house.   The doctor also disliked Mitchell because he drank too much, talked too much, smoked too much, and was irritatingly more popular than the good doctor. On the car ride home he had asked Dorothy, "So, what was so funny about that joke Mitchell told?   I mean anyone could see that punchline coming a mile away." Dorothy was silent except for a hiccup. "You drank too much," he muttered to himself and then added as an afterthought, "again."   As the car pulled into the driveway he recited the punchline to himself, "Anal deficiency."   Dr. Quagmire simply shook his head in disbelief.

Dr. Quagmire parked the car. He and Dorothy walked to the front door.   They stood in the darkness of the front porch while the doctor fumbled with his keys trying to find the right one.   He swore, "Damn it! Why didn't Angie leave the light on?" Dorothy hiccuped again. After fumbling about with the keys and the lock for a while, he managed to unlock the door.

The couple stepped into the hallway, turned on the lights, and there hanging from the ceiling, dangling on the end of a piece of string, at eye level, were two pieces of paper. Dr. Quagmire grabbed them.

The one piece of paper bore Angie Quagmire's signature.   The other piece of paper was a ransom note that was assembled from words and letters cut out of the headlines of newspapers. The message read: *We have your daughter. If you want to see her alive again you must pay us $500,000 by tommorrow at 10:30 pm. We will call you with directions. If you call the pollice she will die.*

"Angie...five hundred...Angie...five hundred thou...sand... Angie," stuttered the doctor as the room went in and out of focus.

"They've misspelled *police*," said Dorothy reading the note a second time. The doctor's legs buckled beneath him. "And *tomorrow* only has one 'm'. Doesn't it?" She turned to Dr. Quagmire for confirmation, but the doctor had already fainted.

Angie is revived

When Angie Quagmire opened her eyes. She saw what appeared to be three faces looking down on her. The light in the room was bad and everything was out of focus. She squinted but it did no good. She tried to move and realized that her legs and hands were tied. "Where am I? Why can't I see?"

"Listen, sweetheart, you'll be back home with Daddy and Mommy in no time," spat Edgar sarcastically. "Once that lousy bastard of a father of yours gives me the money I want, you are free to go. So, I suggest you try to make the best of this situation."

"What have you done to me?" pleaded Angie squinting. "Why can't I see?"

Edgar and Shem left the room, but Jonah lingered behind and admired Angie Quagmire from the shadows as she struggled with the ropes.

She was a young girl that possessed a beauty that was so rare and flawless that most people found it difficult to approach her. She was otherworldly - cursed with an ugly beauty. Angie Quagmire had never been on a date in her entire life for the simple reason that no one could find the courage to talk to her. Boys from her school were satisfied daydreaming about her or fantasizing about her in the locker rooms. For everyone that laid eyes on her, she represented the impossible, the untouchable. Jonah was not unlike most boys, although he would have liked to say something his reservoir of words
46

had suddenly run dry. He simply stood silently watching her.

Steve Mitchell

When Dr. Quagmire opened his eyes, he saw his wife and Steve Mitchell standing over him. Mitchell was holding a fire engine red bucket in his hands that had at one time contained the water, that was now the puddle, in which the doctor laid.

"Are you OK, doc?" asked Mitchell.

"What the hell are you doing here?" Dr. Quagmire said soggy and disoriented.

"Dorothy called me and said that you were out cold and she couldn't bring you around."

Sitting up in the puddle of water, the doctor sighed, "Couldn't you have used a cup of water instead of a bucket?"

"Are you going to be OK, doc?" inquired Mitchell dodging the doctor's question.

"I'm fine. And now, if you don't mind, since you have accomplished what you were called here to do, by dousing me with a bucket of water, please leave."

Steve Mitchell stood stock still. He was irritated with the doctor's abruptness and lack of gratitude. "Listen Harry, I know that you are upset because of Angie…"

"Steve…" exclaimed Dorothy.

The doctor turned on Dorothy like a vicious dog, "You told *him*?" he growled pointing at Mitchell.

"Don't worry doc, we'll get her back safe and sound," reassured Mitchell.

"No." said the doctor confronting him. "That is where you are wrong Mitchell. I'll get her back. Now get the hell out of my house."

Steve Mitchell slowly made his way to the door, dragging his feet. As he was about to exit he turned back to the doctor and said, "Dorothy, if you need anything, you know where to find me."

"You're usually here," shouted the doctor as the door closed behind Mitchell. Then, the doctor, who had a flair for melodrama, picked up the telephone and walked over to Dorothy. "Here you go. Who else do you want to tell? Hmm...Do you want to call your boss from work?"

"I told him because....because...I don't know why. He showed up and I started crying...and you were asleep on the floor," Dorothy shouted back, the tears welling in her eyes.

"I was *passed out* on the floor Dorothy. There's a slight difference between fainting and sleeping." Then the doctor went for the heart, "Listen, let's quit with the games. I know you're screwing that schlep. You probably didn't even call him over. You probably made a rendezvous with him at the party. But poor you, our daughter being kidnapped screwed everything up. Huh? Am I right? Well?"

"Go to hell," Dorothy was crying.

Dr. Quagmire had long believed that his wife was capable of the most heinous infidelities but he had never accused her of anything before. He watched her as she sobbed, but he was not exactly sorry, nor did he feel sad because he had hurt her. He just felt confused.

The couple stood in the hallway in a petrified silence for what felt like an eternity. Lost to one another. Pondering what neither had the courage to say.

Then the phone rang.

The Stockholm Syndrome

Edgar commanded Jonah, "Take the truck and drive it off a cliff!"

Jonah didn't take Edgar seriously, although he was being dead serious. He detested his grandson Gerry to such an extent that he would have liked nothing more than to see one of Gerry's beloved vehicles in a heap of burning metal at the bottom of some ravine. Edgar smiled secretly as he imagined the truck plummeting to it's fiery destruction. Jonah, though, decided he would simply return the vehicle to where he had stolen it from: the lot of *Allen's Courier Service*.

While Jonah was driving he couldn't stop thinking about Angie. Her image had taken over and had rendered all other thoughts trivial and vain. She alone occupied his mind. No matter how he tried to force her out, her image would invariably come floating back again.

At a red light he found himself daydreaming about her. He saw her again in the doorway of her house, the light kissing her skin....When the traffic light turned green, Jonah shook himself from his reveries and reminded himself of the incontrovertible fact that he was her kidnapper. But that voice inside his head, that transparent voice, whispered to him that captives have a tendency to fall in love with, or shall we say have feelings of pity and tenderness for, their captors. Maybe, just maybe, there is a chance after all, Jonah thought optimistically.

Nurse Cheryl Nezwik

Nurse Cheryl Nezwik was greatly concerned that Edgar P. Allen had not checked back into the Relax Palace. She couldn't shake the feeling that something terrible had happened to poor Edgar. What was even worse was that Mrs. Crandall was in remarkably good spirits.

Poor, old Mrs. Crandall had been devastated by the fact Edgar was named *Relax Palace Resident of the Week* for the past 6 weeks. Not only had he broken her unprecedented string of 20 consecutive weeks as Resident of the Week, he seemed determined to keep the title. So, naturally, Nurse Cheryl Nezwik found it strange that the moping and sulking old woman was so jovial.

When Nurse Nezwik asked Mrs. Crandall why she was so happy, the old toothless lady grinned and said, "That bastard Edgar hasn't returned has he?" She cackled wickedly. Nurse Nezwik found this very disturbing. She felt as if she was in a Stephen King horror novel, and Mrs. Crandall's demented laughter was giving her the heebie-jeebies. She scurried from the room, making sure not to take her eyes off Mrs. Crandall. The old woman screamed out after her, "Take his photo off the wall. Take his photo off the wall..."

Nurse Nezwik ran into the central office and quickly thumbed through the Rolodex, looking for Dr. Quagmire's home telephone number. She dialed frantically. "Please pick up...Please pick up...." She whispered into the phone.

The phone was answered after the first ring.

"Hello" said Dr. Quagmire anxiously.

"Dr. Quagmire, this is Cheryl." Her voice trembled and shook with fear, "I'm sorry to bother you so late but it appears that Edgar has been murdered."

"What?" Dr. Quagmire couldn't believe what he heard. First Angie kidnapped and now Edgar murdered? "Oh my god," said an exasperated Dr. Quagmire. "Cheryl, do you know who did it?"

"Mrs. Crandall," she whispered into the phone.

"Mrs. Crandall?" Dr. Quagmire couldn't believe his ears. Mrs. Crandall was a model citizen of the Relax Palace, plus she was pushing ninety and only weighed 70 pounds. "Are you sure it was Mrs. Crandall?"

"Of course. Listen to this," she held the receiver in the direction of the hallway where Mrs. Crandall could still be heard shouting, "Take his picture off the wall."

"Did you hear that?"

"I didn't hear anything."

"She's chanting 'Take his picture off the wall. Take his picture off the wall.' She killed Edgar..."

"How did he die?" sighed Dr. Quagmire. His head was beginning to ache, and he could smell a lawsuit coming.

"I'm not sure," said the frantic Nurse Nezwik.

"What do you mean, you're not sure? Was he pushed down the stairs or maybe he was stabbed? I don't know...are there any telltale signs of murder? Edgar was old. Maybe he died of a heart attack? Maybe it wasn't murder after all," reasoned the doctor.

"Dr. Quagmire, you don't understand," Nurse Nezwik shuddered as the sound of the cackling seemed to get louder. "Oh, my god. I think she's coming after me now."

Dr. Quagmire was confused, tired and frightened. He was also quickly losing his patience. "Nurse Nezwik, where is Edgar's body? In his room? In the TV room?"

"I'm not sure," she cried into the phone. "He never checked back in. Mrs. Crandall probably hired hit men and..."

"He hasn't checked back in?" Dr. Quagmire interrupted her.

"No."

"How do you know he has been murdered?" asked an exasperated Dr. Quagmire.

"Well, I don't know that he has been murdered but I believe..."

51

"Aha, you BELIEVE but you don't KNOW," barked out an infuriated Dr. Quagmire. "Nurse Nezwik," he said composing himself, "I am in the middle of a family crisis and the last thing I need right now are hysterical nurses calling in the middle of the night with stories of murder and Mrs. Crandall," Dr. Quagmire could feel himself losing control again, "So, if Edgar is dead call the police. If you don't know where he is, try contacting his family. Maybe they know where he is. If they don't, then call the police. But do not, and I want to be very clear here, do not CALL ME BACK UNDER ANY CIRCUMSTANCES." Dr. Quagmire slammed down the phone. He had a wild look in his eyes. He was just about to kick the family cat, Clovis, when the phone rang again.

The First Telephone Call

Dr. Quagmire answered the phone and Edgar's voice bucked like a mule from the receiver, "OK, listen. Tomorrow at 10:30 pm you'll go to Fool Runs Creek. There you'll find an envelope in the picnic area. It will contain some directions. Follow them. Once we have the money, the girl goes free."

Dr. Quagmire was still overheated from the call with nurse Nezwik. "We need to talk about the amount of money…" he steamed.

Edgar, though, interrupted him. "No police! If we even sniff a cop the whole thing is off and we'll start sending you pieces of your lovely daughter in the mail. Is that clear?"

"But the amount of money you are asking for is astronomical," said the doctor quietly but forcefully. He didn't want Dorothy to overhear him haggling with the kidnappers.

"It's non-negotiable, Quagmire," spat Edgar viciously.

"How can I be sure that you have Angie and that…," his words stumbled from his mouth, "that…she's…still…alive? If you even touch a hair on her head her head so help me god," the doctor yelled out. He then added with a whisper, "but if she is dead it doesn't make sense that I pay you $500,000."

Edgar found Dr. Quagmire repulsive. He yelled to Angie in the other room, "I've got your Daddy on the phone. Do you want to say anything to him?"

Angie yelled out, "Daddy! Daddy! Don't pay them. These men are idiots. Daddy…"

Edgar hung up the phone and turned to Shem, "Go put a sock in her mouth."

Verse 10 from the Book of Ardiots

Dr. Quagmire was standing, holding the telephone receiver in his hands. His daughter's voice, strained and tired, hit him like a hammer. He was stunned and his eyes welled with tears. Dorothy stood watching him. "What did he say? Is Angie OK?" she asked quietly.

"It was Angie. I heard her. She yelled out," the doctor wept. "She yelled out, 'Daddy don't slay them. Read 10 Ardiots.'"

"What does it mean? Is it some sort of code?" puzzled Dorothy.

Dr. Quagmire, tears rolling down his cheeks, said "The Bible Dorothy, verse 10 from the book of Ardiots – Don't slay them." The doctor, not being a very religious man, was convinced that his daughter was pleading for the lives of her captors. She wanted no harm to come to them even though they had just threatened to chop her into pieces and send her home via the post. "What courage. What bravery. My poor Angie," whispered the doctor.

This is a Kidnapping, not a Picnic

It was late, and Edgar and Shem were both having trouble staying awake. "Tonight the fun begins," Edgar yapped at Jonah with what could only be described as a devilish grin. Edgar explained to Jonah that they would need to do a few jobs in the early evening. Edgar had a plan that would ensure there would be no surprise visit by the police at the drop-off. "So, I suggest we all get some sleep," he announced.

Shem had brought out three sleeping bags and the three men arranged their sleeping areas. After about 5 minutes of laying there, staring at the ceiling, Jonah asked, "What about the girl?"

"What about her?" Edgar was annoyed by the question.

"Have you checked on her? Does she need anything?"

"This is a kidnapping, not a picnic. Get to sleep," said Edgar as he rolled over.

Shem was already snoring. As Jonah laid there staring up at the ceiling, he couldn't keep his mind from wandering off to Angie. He could see her face clearly floating above him. He smiled without knowing why. "Maybe she needs to use the bathroom?"

"Goddamn it," Edgar sat up. "Or maybe she would like her nails done?" he said viciously.

Jonah decided there was no need to say anything else.

"Go to sleep," insisted Edgar.

But Jonah just laid there with his hands behind his head thinking of Angie. He couldn't sleep. Once Edgar was snoring, Jonah, ever so quietly, got out of his sleeping bag, poured a glass of water and tiptoed to Angie's room. He opened the door as slowly as possible so as not to make any noise. In the bedroom Angie was awake. She laid there staring up at him.

"I brought you a glass of water," he whispered to her. He propped her up, took the sock from her mouth and held up the glass so that she could drink. Jonah trembled like the string of a guitar playing a sweet melody.

Courting Angie Quagmire (Part 1)

At 8:00 in the morning, Edgar was up and ready for work. Shem was still sleeping but Jonah's sleeping bag was empty. Edgar scratched his head and wondered where the hell Jonah was. The door to the bedroom was ajar, and Edgar began to boil with rage as he thought about Jonah spending the night with the girl. He poked his head inside and saw that Angie was sleeping alone. There was no sign of Jonah. Edgar simply shook his head and walked over to where Shem was sleeping.

"Shem," barked Edgar. Shem's eyes popped open. "I'm going to arrange a few things. When you see Jonah tell him to go to Fool Runs Creek and wait for me there."

Shem nodded his head and Edgar left.

Edgar couldn't have been gone for 5 minutes when Jonah arrived. He had a couple bags full of doughnuts and three cups of coffee.

Jonah saw that Edgar's sleeping bag was empty. "Shem, where's Edgar? I brought breakfast." Jonah put the food on the table and Shem came over to investigate.

"I didn't know if you take sugar or milk so I bought some milk and here is sugar," he said pulling out packets of sugar from his pockets. Shem had already devoured a doughnut covered with powder sugar. The powder sugar had left a white ring around his mouth.

"Has Edgar left?" Jonah asked nervously.

Shem nodded as he took another doughnut.

Jonah realized he didn't have a moment to lose. "I'll go see if the girl is hungry." He took a cup of coffee and a bag of doughnuts into Angie's room and closed the door behind him.

Angie was sleeping and Jonah began to have second thoughts about waking her. He stood over her mesmerized. He knew that she must be exhausted. But at the same time, he had breakfast for her. He couldn't let this noble gesture go to waste. The entire time he stood in line at Big Fat's doughnuts waiting to place his order he thought about the possible ways she could react to him bringing breakfast. He tended to fixate on the scenario in which Angie would look up at him with her big brown eyes and say, "Thank you. You aren't like the other two. You are kind and sweet." And then she would smile at him. So, in the end, he had no choice. He just had to wake her.

"Angie" he said nudging her awake.

The girl's eyes shot open and she squinted in the direction of Jonah.

"I brought you some breakfast," he blushed holding up a cup of coffee and the doughnuts.

She stared at him without saying a word.

Now, Jonah had something else for her, but he felt embarrassed to give it to her. He was filled with doubts and second guessing. But he had gone this far, what did he have to lose? So, he quickly pulled a small bouquet of dandelions, that he had picked for her, from the bag of doughnuts. Angie had only received flowers from one person before: her father. He had given her roses for her 16th birthday. Jonah had never given flowers to anyone before. She sat motionless. Jonah thrust the flowers at her in a gesture of "go on, take them."

Angie gave Jonah a curious look and then asked, "Did the old

56

man die and leave you his sense of humor?"

Setting up the Drop-off

Later that day, Jonah met up with Edgar at Fool Runs Creek, and it was there that Edgar elaborated on his plan for how the drop-off was to take place. He explained, "Dr. Quagmire is an idiot. One thing we can count on is that he called the police. So, we want to make sure that there are no cops at the drop-off. How do we do that?"

Jonah thought for a split second and then said, "I'm not sure."

"I've got a surefire plan kid. No cop will be anywhere near the drop-off."

Edgar had mapped out a tangled course that ran from Fool Runs Creek to Harpo's Woods. The doctor would arrive at Fool Runs Creek find an envelope that contained directions to another landmark where he would find another envelope that would contain directions to another landmark, so on and so forth, until he would reach Harpo's Woods. Edgar reasoned that no cops would follow Dr. Quagmire because they would be too obvious. Plus Edgar had a few surprises to make sure that any electronic surveillance equipment would be rendered useless. So, Edgar and Jonah spent part of the early evening distributing the envelopes containing the instructions.

The last envelope was to be left at Bum Steer Park. Edgar told Jonah to place it at the foot of the big boulder, known to the locals as *Bubba*, which was just off the main path about 500 feet from the park's entrance.

Jonah rushed down the path and soon found the boulder. He was ready to leave the envelope at Bubba's feet when he began thinking, "What if Dr. Quagmire can't find one of these envelopes? If the money isn't delivered, then Angie won't be set free." The thought of being with Angie for another day was very tempting. Jonah found himself in a moral dilemma. "Is it dishonest for a kidnapper to purposely sabotage a kidnapping?" he asked himself. But such a question seemed morally convoluted and oxymoronic. He became lost in the twisted and knotted scenario he found himself. He was a kidnapper that had a very specific duty to perform, but at the same time his heart begged him for more opportunities to sit and wax romantic with Angie. Jonah sighed. Then he thought about Edgar. He knew that Edgar would probably try to shoot him if he found out that he had sabotaged the kidnapping.

But as a jogger came running past Jonah, the thought came to him like an arrow splitting an apple sitting atop someone's head, "What if someone else were to find an envelope and take it away? Anybody that might pass by could find it." Although the envelopes were usually placed in areas that were generally not well traveled, Jonah felt greatly satisfied with his excuse. So, he walked past Bubba, and found himself at the edge of a slippery slope. Jonah inadvertently, almost accidentally, let the envelope fall from his hands.

Martha My Dear

Martha Frigs, unlike Dr. Quagmire, was a devoutly religious person. She knew the Bible forwards and backwards, and she could have easily told him that there was no Book of Ardiots in the Old or New Testament.

Regardless of Martha's religious inclinations though, her life had recently taken a turn for the worst. Her husband Ron confessed to her one night over a dinner of pork chops, mashed potatoes and applesauce that he was in love with someone else. Martha was devastated. While she wept at the dinner table, Ron could only think about how lovely it would be to have mashed potatoes and applesauce smeared all over his body.

A couple of weeks later Ron moved out and Martha began going to her priest, Father Patrick, for counseling. With his help she began to realize things about Ron that she had never really paid much attention to before. For instance, with the help of Father Patrick she remembered a time, a seemingly innocent event when it first happened, where she found Ron in the kitchen completely naked and covered in whipped cream and pineapple slices. Ron didn't seem too shocked when he realized that Martha had seen him. He simply told her, "I wanted to know what it feels like to be a banana split." At the time it happened, Martha remembered excusing this as just another of Ron's silly jokes. He was always making jokes.

This memory led Martha to another, one that she didn't share with Father Patrick. There was a time when they were making love and Ron asked, "Martha, would you mind making some scrambled eggs?"

"Now ?" she asked in mid climax.

"Could you rub them all over my [CENSORED]" she refused to allow the memory to finish. She couldn't bear the foul word that Ron had used to describe his privates. She remembered being as equally shocked then as she was now.

"But don't you think it is a wee bit strange for a grown man to cover himself in whipped cream?" asked Father Patrick.

"Well, when you put it that way, I guess so," muttered Martha who was disappointed she didn't see these telltale signs that her husband had fallen into the grasp of Satan.

After months of counseling, Martha came to the realization that Ron was a sexual deviant. She began to pray earnestly for his salvation and, of course, for him to return home. But it seemed that Ron had made his choice. He preferred mashed potatoes to his wife.

So, with time, Martha gave up on the idea that Ron would someday return home; she stopped praying for his salvation as well, and her gaze turned inward. Like most people, when they find themselves suffering, Martha began to ask the big question, "Why me?" This led to another question that Martha did not have the theological wherewithal to answer, "Why does God let people suffer?"

During one of their sessions, Father Patrick explained to Martha, "Martha, my dear, there are great many people in the world who suffer much worse than you do. There are people starving to death, there are others that are caught in the middle of wars, there are others that are dying from cancer."

Martha retorted, "But why do people suffer at all? Why doesn't God come down and help those people."

"Remember Martha, that God did 'come down' as you put it. He did walk among us and He did help many people. What happened to Him? Well, we crucified Him."

I didn't crucify Him, thought Martha rather insulted that she would be included among Christ's murderers.

Dissatisfied with Father Patrick's answer she began to search for an explanation herself. The first thought that came to mind was, "Maybe God doesn't stop suffering because there is no God." So, she decided to pray earnestly for God to break the silent treatment he had been giving her all her life. She prayed for a sound, one little peep.

Well it just so happened, on the advice of Father Patrick, she signed up for a weekend retreat. He explained to her that a weekend of prayer and quiet in the Bum Steer Woods would do her good. One evening she decided to take a walk through the woods. As she was

60

walking she began praying earnestly for a sign from God when suddenly an envelope fell from the sky and landed at her feet. She was astonished. She picked up the envelope. There was nothing written on it. She opened it and pulled out the note that it contained. It was a typewritten, simple message, "Take the money and leave it at Mutt's Meteor at Harpo's Woods."

"Thank you God," Martha Frigs cried out.

Dr. Quagmire's Odyssey (Part 1)

Dr. Quagmire made sure that he was at Fool Runs Creek at 10:30 pm exactly. He found that the picnic area was overrun by drunken high school students. The area was lit by the headlights of a car and loud, pounding music boomed from a car radio. Empty beer cans were everywhere, and a couple of boys and girls that had obviously imbibed a little too much were lying face down in the grass. Dr. Quagmire surveyed this scene of debauchery from the parking lot unobserved.

As he walked into the picnic area, Dr. Quagmire was spotted by some of the slightly sober teenagers who immediately warned the others. It was as if an enemy had entered their territory. But in general, everyone seemed too drunk to really care about this middle-aged man invading the picnic area.

Dr. Quagmire began scouring the area for the envelope that the kidnappers had told him he would find there. He looked underneath picnic tables, under rocks, around the trunks of trees but he couldn't find it anywhere. There were only two picnic tables that he hadn't searched yet. They were being used by some of the boys and girls to sit on.

Dr. Quagmire walked over to where the tables were. "Don't

mind me boys and girls. I am just looking for something that I lost earlier today. Do you mind, if I look under this table here?"

Most of the group were too caught up competing with one another for the title of *The Most Disenchanted and Troubled Youth* to be bothered by some silly man. They rolled their eyes and sighed at the doctor and his silly quest.

The doctor smiled awkwardly, dropped to his hands and knees, and peered underneath the table. He spotted the envelope stapled to its underside. As he reached out to grab it, he felt something poking him in the back. He looked over his shoulder and saw a boy built like a wall. He was enormous, wide and solid. He was holding a beer in his hands. "Do you a want beer, dude?"

"No thanks," said the doctor.

He pulled the envelope from the table and stood up. The Wall was still standing there, "Come on dude, just one beer."

"No, I have to be going, but thank you any…" A young boy sitting on the table suddenly stood up, staggered and fell towards the doctor. The doctor caught the boy in his arms, and the boy vomited.

When the boy finished retching he collapsed in the grass. The doctor's pants and shoes were covered in vomit.

"Just one beer," begged the Wall.

Back at the Shack

At the shack, while Shem and Edgar were playing poker, Jonah was pacing nervously. He was a turmoil of mixed emotions. He bitterly accused himself of betraying Edgar, but at the same time he blushed with delight when he thought about spending more time with Angie. Jonah was also afraid. If Edgar discovered that he was behind this act of sabotage, he would beat Jonah senseless, or worst yet, kick him off the kidnapping.

"Stop pacing," snapped Edgar. "You're driving me crazy."

"Maybe you and Shem should go, I'm not feeling so hot," complained Jonah grasping his gut.

Edgar regarded Jonah coldly. He peered at him over his hand of cards. He remembered the night of the kidnapping and the mess Jonah had almost made of it with his nervousness.

"If you go anywhere near that girl while we're gone..." Edgar began the threat but he knew he didn't need to complete it. Jonah understood.

Jonah continued to pace, feeling a little relieved that he wouldn't be standing at Edgar's side while he waited for Dr. Quagmire, who would never show up.

Dr. Quagmire's Odyssey (Part 2)

Dr. Quagmire ran to his car and jumped inside. He opened the envelope and began to read the note. "Drive north to Drifter Ridge Court. Drive east on..." The doctor stopped reading because the stench of the vomit was too much for him. He opened the window and put his head out for fresh air. After taking a few deep breaths he continued reading, "Drive east on Drifter Ridge until you come to Hobo's bridge..." Again the doctor needed air. He opened the car door and stumbled out, nearly vomiting himself. The odor was too much for him. So, he kicked off his shoes and quickly pulled off his pants. He threw his pants in the trunk, tried his best to scrape the vomit off his shoes and climbed back into the car. "...until you come to Hobo's bridge. There you will find another envelope."

Dr. Quagmire floored the gas pedal, and his car exploded out of the parking lot and down the road towards Drifter Ridge Court.

Edgar and Jonah had planted 15 envelopes in total, and the doctor spent a solid two hours racing from one place to another picking up envelopes, always hoping that the next would tell him where to deliver the money.

After the 13th envelope the doctor was beginning to get frustrated. He began to think that this was some sort of sadistic joke. He jumped into his car, opened the envelope and read, "Drive to Bum Steer Lane. Take Bum Steer lane to the Raw Deal Bridge. Park your car at the Bridge. Take the money and swim across the river. On the other side you will find another envelope."

He shook his head in disbelief. He was going to have to swim across the Raw Deal River? They had to be kidding.

Anyway, he drove out to the Raw Deal Bridge. He grabbed the bag of money from the backseat and stumbled down the embankment to the river. He waded into the river holding the bag high over his head. But, suddenly the bottom of the river dropped off and he was completely underwater. He swam to the surface trying to keep the bag dry, but it was no good. As he struggled to swim with the bag, it went under the water. The doctor fought his way across the river and crawled out of the river on his hands and knees, dragging the bag of money along behind him.

He took a moment's respite before searching for the next envelope. The envelope proved easy enough to find. It sat in plain sight in a patch of weeds on the river bank. He opened it and the note read, "Follow the river until you come to the main pathway. Take the main path towards the park entrance. 500 feet from the entrance you will find a large boulder. You will find the last envelope at the boulder."

"Thank god", exclaimed Dr. Quagmire relieved that the

nightmare was coming to an end.

The Drop-Off

Edgar and Shem finished their hand of cards and then drove out to the drop-off point. Edgar didn't expect the doctor for another hour or so; they had plenty of time. But he wanted to make sure that he was there early enough so that there wouldn't be any surprises.

Edgar parked the Blue Dodge Eris, and he and Shem walked up the path to Mutt's Meteor. Edgar saw that there was a small black case sitting at base of the rock. He was stupefied. How could the doctor have made the delivery so quickly? It was impossible.

Edgar quickly snatched the bag and opened it. He saw that it contained money. He and Shem hurried back to the car as fast as their old, spindly legs could take them. "It can't be possible. He's quicker than I thought," he panted to Shem.

Inside the car Edgar opened the bag and said gleefully, "He must be desperate to have his little girl back." Because the bag was small, Edgar expected to find large denominations. He expected 100 dollar bills. To his surprise he saw mainly 20s, and a few 5s and some 10 dollar bills. Edgar pulled out the money out and counted it. He counted $3,253.

"I knew that son of a bitch was cheap but what the hell does he think he is doing? Paying us in installments?" Edgar floored the gas pedal and the car shrieked and fishtailed its way out of the parking lot.

Dr. Quagmire's Odyssey (Part 3)

The doctor had been stumbling along in utter darkness for some time. He couldn't see a thing, and he began to think that he must have missed the path that led to the boulder. "Why does this have to

65

be so damn difficult?" he sulked. He was wet and cold and he just wanted this kidnapping to end.

The doctor decided to trudge on and if he didn't come across the main path in the next couple minutes, he would turn around and look for it. Then he heard what sounded like voices up ahead. He immediately thought that it must be the kidnappers, and he scurried behind a tree.

There were two men, they had flashlights and were shining the lights this way and that. As they walked by the doctor, he could hear them talking to one another.

"How much did they want for the place?"

"$355,000. "

Dr. Quagmire looked down at the soggy bag that held *his* money.

"Well, what can I do? Jenny really likes the place…and…"

"So you're going to buy it, huh?"

"What about you?"

"Well you know that …"

"Well, I suggest you save your money. You're going to need it to pay the hospital bill when they remove this bag from your ass," said Dr. Quagmire as he stepped out from the behind the tree twirling the black bag over his head as if it were some sort of medieval weapon.

The men quickly turned towards the doctor and pointed their flashlights at his face. He was blinded as he rushed at them. He lowered his shoulder and plowed into the men he believed were the kidnappers. The three men were caught in a screaming, grunting, pounding, bleeding, spitting, clothes ripping hurricane of human violence. After a solid 20 seconds of fighting, the doctor pulled himself from the fray. The other two men pointed their flashlights at Dr.

Quagmire. "What in the hell do you think you're doing?" asked one of the men.

Then one of the men shined his flashlight on something that the other was holding in his hand. It was a badge. These men were police officers. "Do you know that you just assaulted two police officers?" the man holding the badge asked.

"I am so sorry officer. I thought you were somebody else."

"Where are your pants?" the other demanded.

Dr. Quagmire had forgotten that he wasn't wearing any pants.

"I had an accident," he replied.

"What kind of accident?"

"Some one threw up on me," Dr. Quagmire, feeling that the explanation of someone vomiting on him needed clarification so he elaborated, "There were some kids drinking at Bum Steer Park..."

"You were at Bum Steer Park earlier?" interrupted one of the officers.

"What were you doing there?" said the other

"Were you wearing your pants then?"

The doctor didn't like where this was going. He felt that his arrest was imminent. So, without further ado, he took to his heels. The police chased after him yelling, "Stop or we'll shoot." But the doctor kept running. He believed that being shot was a far better alternative than being caught.

The three men raced through the woods, the police officers with their guns in their hands hoping for a clear shot at the doctor. Suddenly the doctor broke from the path and jumped into the river. The policemen followed him to the edge of the river. One of the officers jumped in and started swimming after him.

The doctor quickly reached the other side and pulled himself out of the water panting and gasping for air. The officer was close behind. The doctor picked up a good sized stone and threw it. Bullseye. The officer grabbed his face screaming. His partner, standing on the riverbank shouted out, "Bill, are you OK?" The doctor sprinted to his car. He was sure he could hear sirens as he sped down the road.

Courting Angie Quagmire (Part 2)

Once Edgar and Shem left, Jonah tried to work up the courage to enter Angie's room. The flowers and breakfast earlier in the morning, weren't received so well. Jonah stood outside the door listening to the absolute silence that emanated from Angie's room. The only thing he could hear was his own breathing. He told himself, that all he had to do was push open the door, and that once he crossed the threshold, once he had taken the first steps, things would become easier. Jonah hesitated for another moment and then threw the door open impulsively. The door banged against the wall. Angie was startled and looked up, her face was distorted with fear. Jonah stood in the doorway holding a candle and a small portable radio.

"Angie," said Jonah softly from the doorway.

"What?"

"Do you want anything?" He took a few nervous steps into the room.

"No."

"Do you want to hear some music?"

"No."

"Are you sure? I brought you a radio." Jonah held up the radio so that Angie would be sure to see it. She sat listlessly on the bed.

68

"Are your eyes better?"

"Yes."

"How many fingers am I holding up?" Jonah playfully held up two fingers.

"Two."

Jonah was beginning to feel proud. The conversation seemed to be going well. He turned on the radio and began scanning for something he liked. He stopped at a station, "There, that's nice, don't you think?"

"Yeah," said Angie devoid of emotion.

"I like this song too. Do you know it?"

"No."

"It's a Beach Boys song," he said. In fact the song was *Wouldn't it be Nice* by the Beach Boys. As the eternal boys of summer harmonized about how cool it would be to get married, Jonah asked, "Are you sure you don't want anything to eat or drink?"

"Yes."

"Yes you are sure? Or yes you would like something to eat?"

Angie snapped. "Would you stop asking me so many questions. My god, you are like some little kid always asking a million questions. Leave me alone." She turned away from Jonah.

Jonah felt as if Angie had just plunged a metal stake into his heart. He had put himself in grave danger by sabotaging the kidnapping so that he could spend some quality time with her, and she obviously wasn't interested. He couldn't understand what he had done to deserve this.

"Are you angry because you've been kidnapped?" he asked innocently.

Angie said nothing. She just glared defiantly at him.

The Second Telephone Call

Dr. Quagmire returned home shortly after midnight. He arrived in a state of frenzied, hysterical panic. He raced through the front door of his house and into the living room. Dorothy and Steve Mitchell were waiting for him.

"Where have you been?" asked Dorothy anxiously. The doctor said nothing. He was scared. Everything had gone wrong. He didn't even greet Mitchell's presence with his usual vehemence. He simply ignored him.

"Where are your pants?" asked Dorothy.

"Did they call?" asked the doctor desperately.

"Yes and they were furious. They said that you were $496,747 short."

"What?" the doctor was baffled.

"Why are you so wet?" asked Mitchell chewing on a pretzel stick.

"Why are you here?" the doctor was beginning to become enraged.

"I've brought someone I want you to meet," replied Mitchell with a wink.

The doctor was about to attack Mitchell when the phone rang. He snatched up the phone and said, "Yes."

"Listen you stupid bastard," the voice from the telephone growled. "Is this your idea of a joke? We ask for $500,000 and instead you gave us $3,253? Let me tell you something, the girl is as good as dead."

"No, please don't hurt her," begged the doctor. "I don't know what you are talking about. I never dropped off the money. The police were at the park. I never found the last envelope."

70

"I told you no police Quagmire…" Edgar was enraged.

"No, you don't understand. The police were at the park and they kicked me out. I couldn't deliver the money. I have it with me," the doctor explained frantically.

Edgar was confused. If the doctor didn't leave the money, then who did and why? Who was the money intended for? But then Edgar thought, maybe this is some sort of trick. "Tomorrow at 11:30 at Mutt's meteor in Harpo's Park. Be there with the money."

"Please…will I have to go hunting for envelopes again? If so, I need to…" Edgar hung up the phone.

"So, what happened?" asked Jonah nervously.

"I smell a rat," said Edgar staring off into the distance, lost in deep thought.

"Oh, really?" said Jonah turning away from Edgar hoping to conceal his guilt, which he believed was as visible as an albatross hanging from his neck.

Edgar dumped the money from the satchel on the table and pulled apart the little sack. Edgar searched for some sort of tiny tracking device. He found nothing.

"I don't trust Quagmire. This is some sort of psychological warfare," said Edgar staring off into the distance. Edgar didn't know what the doctor was planning, but he knew it was something rotten. He wanted desperately to beat the doctor at his own game, whatever that may be. What could he do to retaliate? Edgar fumed, and he thought, but he could come up with nothing. He became lost in fantasies of torturing Quagmire.

"What can I do to Quagmire?" he mumbled to himself.

Jonah, overhearing the faintly uttered question, responded, "Maybe we should keep the girl?"

Edgar turned to Jonah and said with a malignant frown, "Don't be ridiculous. Not a word to the girl. Let her believe that her precious father is paying for her in installments."

Angie, hearing that her father was paying for her in installments, began to quietly sob in the bedroom. She couldn't understand why her father had only paid $3,253. If he was paying the ransom in installments of $3,253 like the kidnappers had said, then she would have to be with the kidnappers for another 150.7 days she calculated. She buried her face in the pillow and wept.

Jonah, though, was relieved that things had turned out as badly as they did. He was free from suspicion, and he had just gained a little more time to steal Angie Quagmire's heart.

Hang on to your Ego

When Dr. Quagmire put the phone down, he glared at Steve Mitchell. He had the uncontrollable urge to strangle him. Mitchell saw the deranged look of violence in the doctor's face and carefully backed away from him.

"Harry, I want to help," he protested. "I've brought someone here to talk to you." Mitchell ran behind a sofa. Now there was furniture serving as a barrier between the two men.

"Harry, stop it. Steve is just trying to help us," Dorothy protested grabbing the doctor by the arm. But Dr. Quagmire had become overtaken with the desire to do physical harm to Steve Mitchell. If it meant murder, so be it. He shook his arm free from Dorothy's grasp.

"This guy is a miracle worker," Mitchell was trying hard to persuade the doctor to listen to him, but Dr. Quagmire was out of reach. He was calmly and patiently pursuing Mitchell as he ran around the sofa.

Suddenly, music started playing. The doctor stopped and listened. He tried to determine where the music was coming from.

He walked towards the kitchen. Through the doorway he could see a strange man sitting at the kitchen table. He was as pale as the moon, with white blond hair tied in a ponytail, dressed completely in black and from his shoulders hung a navy blue cape. Laying on the table in front of the man was a small radio type of device. The doctor couldn't recognize the song that crackled from the plastic box. He stood in the kitchen doorway observing the stranger who sat motionless. The song finished and the strange man reached out and turned off the device.

"We are made to play many games all our lives, and the most dangerous game we can play is the game called Fear, doctor," he said cryptically, as if he were a prophet predicting the imminent end of the world.

Jimmy "the Shade" Shade

The man sitting in Dr. Quagmire's kitchen was Jimmy "the Shade" Shade, and Jimmy Shade was the type of person that believed *Intelligence equals Eccentricity*. Simply put, intelligent people would do things like wear socks on their hands while at home in order to avoid having to touch metal (silverware or doorknobs, etc.) So, Jimmy Shade indulged and nurtured his eccentricities so that everyone would clearly understand he was extremely intelligent.

Jimmy Shade spent his days in his apartment writing. He had written two books. His first was a cheery little number titled *The Mass Extinction Event*. This book began with the sentence, "The greatest conspiracy of all is that there is no conspiracy." After the first

73

sentence, though, the book went downhill fast. The local paper, the **Eye of Ersatz**, gave it a rather merciless review, "This book is the incomprehensible work of an ass, and I don't mean the kind that lives on a farm." The book, though, was moderately successful.

His second book was *How to Change your Life Using Pop Music*. This book was disguised as a self-help book but it turned out to be a philosophical treatise on whether an objective criteria exists to classify the subjective effects of music on a listener. This book, unlike his first, began with someone else's words (although Leonard Cohen was not given credit for the statement, it belonged to him) "The Nazis were overthrown by music."

This book was far from successful but Jimmy Shade lived by its credo. Wherever he went he had a radio-cd-mp3 player device (or RCM3 for short) that he would use to provide spontaneous soundtracks, or "autoschediastracks" as he called them, in order to provide a certain emotive resonance to an experience as it occurred. This is precisely what he did when he played the Beach Boys' *Hang on to Your Ego* in Dr. Quagmire's kitchen.

When not writing, Jimmy Shade was either getting drunk or moonlighting as a Private Investigator or both. He liked thinking of himself as a crime fighter, someone helping to balance the moral check book of the universe, if you will. So he spent some evenings spying on cheating husbands and wives documenting their infidelities and betrayals, or spying on people that had made insurance claims in order to verify that their alleged injuries were not faked.

But business was not generally good for Jimmy Shade. Perhaps it was because he always dressed in black leotards? Perhaps because he wore a cape? Or maybe it was due to the fact that his office never opened until the sun had set? Whatever the reason, Jimmy

74

Shade had only a few customers. Steve Mitchell had been one of them.

Steve Mitchell and the Shade

Steve Mitchell had called Jimmy Shade for help one cloudy and aching morning. The night before, Mitchell had been partying with his good friend Hank and the two had participated in an evening of wild and obscene decadence. When Mitchell woke up, the only thing he could remember about the night before was that he couldn't remember anything. But judging by the way he felt, it was clear that he had over done it. He sat up and felt awful. His head pounded with a ferocious violence that made him feel nauseous. Checking his watch, he saw that the hour was quickly approaching 2:00 in the afternoon. His estranged wife was due in an hour. Mitchell, his wife and their toy poodle, Kimmy, had an appointment at the dog psychiatrist at 3:30. Just the thought of the dog psychiatrist made Mitchell implode with anger. "Stupid damn dog," he said as he collapsed back into the bed.

Now, Kimmy was no ordinary pet. She was a celebrity, and she had been in 55 commercials in the 4 years since she became a professional dog actor. She had advertised everything from dog toys to Poodey Poodles potty-training kits. But Mitchell's wife believed their recent relationship problems were affecting Kimmy adversely. She just wasn't as performative on the sets as she used to be, hence the psychiatrist.

Mitchell pulled the covers over his head, stretched out and tried to make himself comfortable. He closed his eyes and took deep breaths. It was then that he had a sudden and terrifying realization. Something small, hard, furry and cold was at his feet. He pulled the covers back slowly and gasped. Kimmy, feet pointing straight into the air, laid at the end of the bed extremely dead.

"No," choked Mitchell as he raced on his hands and knees to Kimmy. "Oh, my god." He poked the dog. She was petrified. He sat above the dog and continued to repeat the words *Oh, my god*, but this was because the sudden rush of movement made him feel as though his brain was ready to explode. He felt truly miserable.

He laid back down in the bed and wondered what his wife would say. Then Mitchell began to wonder what *he* was going to say. How was *he* going to explain Kimmy's death? He couldn't remember a thing from the night before, and then a rather horrifying thought struck him. "Oh, my god," he cringed.

Why was the dog in my bed? Could I have, Mitchell stopped thinking and ran to the bathroom, knelt at the toilet and cried like a baby, "Oh, my god."

After vomiting, Mitchell felt a little better and he tried to be optimistic. Things weren't as bad as they seemed. Maybe the dog simply died? Maybe it was a heart attack? There was no evidence that anything out of the ordinary had happened. But when Mitchell reentered the bedroom and saw Kimmy, her little feet pointing to the ceiling, he felt strangely guilty, and he began to panic. His impulse to flee kicked in, so he started to get dressed. As he grabbed socks from his sock drawer he also inadvertently pulled out a business card. The card fell to the floor. Mitchell picked it up and read it.

Jimmy the Shade Shade

Detective / Novelist

I can help you solve your problems whether they are real or fictional

(258) 741-1590

He had no idea who this Jimmy Shade person was or why he

had his business card. But he needed help and this card was offering a lifeline to him. Mitchell couldn't refuse. He stumbled to the telephone and desperately dialed the number.

"Hello," said a sleepy, groggy voice.

"Is this Jimmy the Shade Shade?" asked Mitchell on the verge of tears.

"Yes, who is this?"

"I need help," said Mitchell breaking down.

"I only work at night," explained the Shade.

"But my," the word *dog* stuck in Mitchell's throat. He was blubbering uncontrollably. "Kimmy is dead," he finally managed to say.

Jimmy Shade was silent. He was thinking how he could handle this situation profitably. "OK, I might be able to help you, but it's going to cost," he thought of a number and the first to come to mind was, "$5,000."

"No problem," Mitchell said relieved that Jimmy Shade, whoever he was, was willing to take on the burden of helping him conceal his guilt.

Jimmy Shade took down Mitchell's address and told him he would be over in ten minutes. Mitchell hung up the phone and began to meditate on the mysterious Jimmy Shade and why he had his business card. Thinking wasn't one of Mitchell's strong points, and, so, after only a couple minutes of concentrated effort, he gave up.

Jimmy Shade arrived promptly, and as soon as Mitchell saw him walking to the front door he remembered the strange man in the tights and cape from one of Hank's parties. He remembered Hank had introduced Jimmy Shade by saying something like, "This guy is a real life saver." Mitchell felt a wave of relief wash over him.

He ran to meet Jimmy Shade and the two discussed Kimmy. Jimmy Shade, had not understood that Kimmy was a dog and was a bit irritated that he had rushed to help Mitchell. The problem was simple. "Just put the dog on it's mat or something. Say you found it there."

"I can't do that. My wife will probably want an autopsy," protested Mitchell.

"So?"

Mitchell imagined being at a veterinarian's office. The vet would walk out of an operating room and stroll up to him and his wife and ask, "Mr. and Mrs. Mitchell, we need to talk about what happened on the night Kimmy died." Mitchell felt sick and replied testily, "So, we need another plan."

Jimmy Shade thought for a moment and then said, "We'll make it look like your wife killed the dog."

"How?"

Jimmy Shade made it sound so simple. Since Mrs. Steven Mitchell was on her way home from somewhere, and since she was driving a car, all they needed to do was make it look as if she ran the dog over.

"How?"

"We throw the dog under the car as she drives by," he said effortlessly.

So, that is what the two men planned. Mitchell, still in his bathrobe grabbed a rake from the garage and was pretending, rather ineptly, to be doing yard work. Jimmy Shade, in the cover of the large oak in the front yard, would pop out as the car would pass by and toss Kimmy at the tires. It was a desperate plan - one that redefined the term fool proof. It was proof that both men were fools.

The men waited at their stations, Mitchell with his rake and

Jimmy Shade behind the tree. The men waited silently, like soldiers waiting to ambush the enemy. Mitchell gazed down the road looking for his wife's car. After a couple minutes of tense anticipation, Mitchell announced, "OK, here she comes."

Jimmy Shade prepared himself. He took out his RCM3 and pushed play. The Beatles' *Day Tripper* started. He held the dog as if it were a bowling ball and waited for the word.

Mitchell, slightly confused by the sudden sound of the opening guitar riff from *Day Tripper,* tried to decipher where the music was coming from. His distraction almost cost the men their window of opportunity. But Mitchell saw, from the corner of his eye, the white of the steel belted radials passing. "Now," he yelled.

Jimmy Shade rolled the dog. His form was perfect but he grossly miscalculated the size of Steve Mitchell's yard. The dog rolled to a stop 3 feet from the street. Gutterball.

"Oh, my god," yelled Mitchell, and in a single fluid motion, he ran, dove for the dog and tossed it at the car. Kimmy hit the windshield and bounced off and landed in the street. Mitchell's wife screamed, pulled hard at the steering wheel and smashed into the parked car of their neighbor.

Mitchell ran to the wreck and greeted his wife, tapping on the driver side window, "You killed Kimmy. You ran over the dog."

Mrs. Steven Mitchell pushed open the door and emerged from the smoke, broken glass and crumpled metal of the accident. She staggered to where Kimmy laid in the road. "Something hit the window," she said to Steve, her eyes full of tears.

"You killed Kimmy," Steve repeated his earlier accusation.

At that moment, Jimmy Shade walked out from behind the oak, his RCM3 blaring the Beatles, and said, "I want my money Mitchell."

"Who's he?" asked Mrs. Steven Mitchell a little shocked by Jimmy Shade's superheroesque attire.

"That is Jimmy the Shade. He's a bona fide miracle worker," said Mitchell with a grin.

The Shade's Plan

"Who is this bozo?" asked Dr. Quagmire.

Steve Mitchell immediately came to Jimmy Shade's defense and said, "This is no clown. This is the Shade. Jimmy 'the Shade' Shade." He said this as if this statement alone was sufficient argument to justify Jimmy Shade's presence. "This is the guy I was trying to tell you about. He is the answer to all your problems."

"Mitchell, right now you're my only problem," yelled the doctor.

"Bring me the ransom note," interrupted Jimmy Shade.

"Bring you the ransom note?" chortled Dr. Quagmire. "Who do you think you are?"

"I told you, he is Jimmy 'the Shade' Shade," said Mitchell with emphasis on 'the Shade' part of the name.

"Could you have come up with a more redundant nickname?" asked Dr. Quagmire with what he considered fiery wit.

Jimmy Shade remained silent. It was Dr. Quagmire's wife that responded. "Harry, maybe this guy can help us."

Dr. Quagmire wanted to yank this Jimmy Shade up from his chair by his ears and throw him through the kitchen window. Dorothy, though, handed Jimmy Shade the ransom note.

Jimmy Shade read it over and then handed it back to her. He then sat for a moment, silently collecting his thoughts. "The kidnappers, there is more than one, are men. They are also amateurs.

This is probably their first kidnapping."

Mitchell was very impressed, "Isn't that amazing? He can tell all that from a ransom note. Anything else?"

"They aren't proficient spellers," Jimmy Shade added dryly.

Dr. Quagmire was not impressed. "Why do I need you? You didn't tell us anything we didn't already know."

"And how do you know they are men?" asked Dorothy eagerly.

"Men, usually write very threatening letters. Plus the language is very phallocentric," responded Jimmy Shade.

"This guy is amaz..." began Mitchell. "What a crock of..." interrupted the doctor. "So, have there been women kidnappers?" Dorothy's question silenced the doctor prematurely.

"Of course," said Jimmy Shade.

"So how the hell are you going to help us?" he doctor asked incredulously.

"Well, first and foremost your daughter is still alive. They won't be able to kill her. They aren't the killing type. They just want to make a fast buck. So, I suggest we do something that will throw them out of their game."

"Like what?" prompted Mitchell.

"You won't make the payment," said Jimmy Shade dryly.

"Sorry there Shade, but I beat you to that one. I already missed the payment tonight."

Jimmy Shade sat quietly and had a faraway look in his eyes.

"He means you have to miss *this* payment as well," said Mitchell.

"Listen," the doctor said seating himself at the kitchen table across from Jimmy Shade, "I am going to pay these bastards and get my daughter back. Thanks, but no thanks."

Jimmy Shade remained motionless.

"They threatened to cut her into pieces and send her home via the mail," the doctor said trying to elicit a reaction from Jimmy Shade.

"I see your point. If they send her through the mail there is a good chance parts of her will be lost or delivered to the wrong address."

Although, Dr. Quagmire did not appreciate Jimmy Shade's macabre attempt at humor, he was exhausted and was beginning to think sloppily. One such sloppy thought that entered his mind was, Maybe this guy can help me get Angie back without losing a cent. The idea of getting his daughter back for nothing offset Dr. Quagmire's low opinion of Jimmy "the Shade" Shade. Maybe I should give this clown a chance, thought the doctor imprudently.

The Morning News

Martha Frigs was reading the local newspaper, **The Eye of Ersatz**, and the headline on the front page read, *Deranged man without pants attacks police in park.* What is the world coming to? she asked herself, not expecting an answer but more as a statement of shock. Pantless men in parks attacking police seemed almost unthinkable.

But Martha had better things to do rather than puzzle over the deterioration of modern society. She wanted to go back to the park in order to speak to God. After cleaning out her bank account and leaving it at Mutt's Meteor she needed some direction. Specifically, she needed some financial advice. How was she supposed to pay the electric bill?

So, she drove to Harpo's Park and strolled to Mutt's Meteor. She was expecting some sort of answer. She was expecting something.

She saw that the satchel containing her savings was gone. She started to pray for advice when she saw a strange sight. She saw what appeared to be a man, dressed in black with a long navy blue cape, shielding himself from the sun with a large black umbrella. He was about 50 feet from her and he was walking slowly and deliberately towards her. Martha sat motionless. She saw that he was as pale as a skeleton and wore sunglasses.

Soon this apparition (she no longer thought of this thing walking through the woods as a man) was standing in front of her. She was convinced that standing before her was death incarnate.

"Please, I don't want to die," she cringed. She closed her eyes and began to pray. When her husband Ron had moved out she had prayed many nights for death but she was always insincere. She didn't want to actually die. She was just a bit down, a bit overloaded with worries perhaps. Things weren't working out as she wanted. She wasn't getting enough sleep. She did not want to die.

Suddenly, a noise emerged from the apparition. It was music, a song she had heard before. It was a Beach Boys song, at least it sounded like the Beach Boys. Without looking up, she listened.

The melancholic sounds of *God Only Knows What I'd Be Without You* wafted from Jimmy Shade's RCM3. Martha stood transfixed to the spot. This strange and deathlike being had brought her a message: God knew her pain.

Slowly the music grew fainter and fainter until it was no longer audible. She looked up and the apparition was gone. Martha knew exactly what she was supposed to do.

Courting Angie Quagmire (Part 3)

Jonah had attempted to scale the mountains surrounding Angie Quagmire's heart, but to no avail. He was lost in the crags and cliffs, at the end of his rope, and was nowhere near her heart. He needed more time. But time was difficult to be had since Edgar was always around. Jonah did not dare enter Angie's room while Edgar was there. So, he waited patiently for his next opportunity, which came precisely at 1:30 in the afternoon when Edgar announced that he was going out to buy lunch. Shem stayed behind, and as soon as the door closed behind Edgar, Jonah jumped from his seat and quickly made his way to Angie's room. He stopped at the door and said to Shem as he entered the room, "I'll just check on the girl."

Inside the room he could hear Angie crying. He walked over to her and asked, "What's wrong?"

At first Angie didn't say anything. She just laid there. Jonah wanted to reach out and touch her, to try to comfort her in some way. Suddenly, Angie's voice rose from the bed, "Is it true?"

"What?" he asked tenderly.

"My father wants to pay for me in installments?" she sobbed.

Jonah didn't know what to say. He was again faced with a moral dilemma. His initial inclination was to tell her the truth. But Edgar had been very clear, Angie was not to know that there was some sort of mix-up with the money.

He sat there silently weighing the pros and cons when Angie said, "I can't believe it. My own father...and I thought..." she began to weep.

Jonah couldn't bear the sobbing and he whispered to her, "Angie, I think there was some sort of mix-up, that's all."

"What do you mean Jonah?" Angie asked raising her head

from the mattress.

"You know my name," Jonah declared. He saw this as a clear sign that he was not as far from her heart as he had calculated.

Martha's Plan

After her encounter with Death at Mutt's Meteor, Martha came to the conclusion that she needed to "re-engineer" her life. She needed to regain control. She needed to do something that would put her back in the proverbial driver's seat. So, she devised a plan. Step 1 of this plan entailed getting a message to her ex-husband Ron.

Martha, like most people, tended to make very simple things complicated; therefore, she labored over how she would get a message to him. Since she had met most of Ron's co-workers at company picnics and office parties she felt uncomfortable with the idea of delivering the message herself. She did not want Ron to know that the message was from her. She needed an anonymous person to deliver the message. She thought about enlisting the help of Father Patrick, but he had been advising her to forget about Ron completely. She then began to wonder about who else she could employ to deliver her message when suddenly she realized that the problem was simple. She would create an email account and send it to him via email. So, Martha registered the address scrambledeggs@hotmail.com. She thought this would get her ex-husband's attention. The message was simple

Dearest Ron,

I am your secret admirer. I have been watching you for some time and I like what I see. I have something for you. Cum to Mutt's Meteor at midnight tonight.

Love and XXX
ScrambledEggs

Mr. George Pung

Ron's boss, Mr. George Pung, was slightly taller than a seven year old child, with a round face and belly, and dark eyes. He was hairstyle challenged. The few strands of hair that still grew from his head were kept long. Mr. Pung seemed to believe that the length of his hair compensated for his lack. But to most he simply looked ridiculous.

Mr. Pung did not believe in what he called "secrecy." Now Mr. Pung's notion of "secrecy" was very similar to what other people think of as "privacy." But Mr. Pung would take shelter in the argument that since he was the supervisor he had a right to see what his employees were saying since they rarely spoke to him. So, he monitored their emails and every now and again he would find something really juicy.

It just so happened that he had monitored Ron for sometime, and he didn't like what he read. Ron's behavior was weird, and it bugged him. Mr. George Pung was fed up with Ron. The day that his IT minions handed him an email from someone with address of scrambled eggs, Mr. Pung decided, then and there, that he would fire Ron.

He called Ron into his office. Ron entered smiling, not knowing that he was entering the lion's den. Mr. Pung told Ron point blank, "Mr. Frigs, you are fired."

"What?" gasped Ron. "Why?"

"Because I am the boss and I don't like you," grunted the little man.

"What have I done? I mean, you can't fire me just because you don't like me."

"Sure I can," smiled Mr. Pung.

"I'll get a lawyer," Ron threatened turning red with anger.

"If you involve a lawyer I'll make sure you never find work again. I am a very powerful man in this town, very influential, and I know things about you Mr. Frigs that are very damaging."

"Like what?" Ron demanded angrily.

"Like scrambled eggs," said Mr. Pung with a self satisfied smile.

Ron was confused by the reference to *scrambled eggs*, but the only thing he could imagine was that Martha had told Mr. Pung about the scrambled eggs. How else could he know? "You're screwing my ex-wife, aren't you?" Ron accused.

"What?" now it was Mr. Pung's turn to gasp. The tables had turned. Mr. Pung was in fact screwing a married woman every Thursday afternoon. Was this woman Ron's ex-wife? The men sat there in a stalemate, glaring at each other, separated by Mr. Pung's cheap, fake wooden desk.

So it was that Ron was fired, then re-hired, and then he quit. Ron threatened as he left, "Mr. Pung, I will see you in court." As Ron walked out of the office and into the bright and glorious sunlight of a summer day, the invitation to meet his "secret admirer" slipped away forever.

Let What You Do be Done In Love

"This disaster is going to end tonight," Edgar barked at Jonah, Shem and Angie as if he were some deranged drill sergeant instructing his recruits. This time the drop-off was going to be much simpler. The kidnappers would take Angie with them and once they had the money she would be set free. No more envelopes, no more games.

Jonah was untying Angie's hands and feet and as he was bent over her, he looked into her eyes. She stared blankly back. He wondered if she could feel the fireworks exploding between them. But there was something profoundly sad about this moment. This was their goodbye. He was untying her and she was going free.

"For the love of god kid, get a move on. We need to do this tonight," Edgar was angry and anxious.

Once Angie was untied she was ushered into the car at gunpoint. Edgar sat in the passenger seat, Shem climbed into the backseat with the girl, and Jonah drove.

They drove to Harpo's woods and as they entered the parking area Edgar instructed Jonah, "Drive the car up that foot path." Jonah did as he was told and the trail soon opened into an area that contained a strange rock formation known as Mutt's Meteor. Legend had it that if you looked carefully at the rock you could discern a dog, perhaps a shar-pei. Jonah parked the car.

Edgar checked his watch. It was 10:30. "In one hour sweetie-pie you'll be home with Mommy and Daddy."

The car was silent as the kidnappers and Angie waited for Dr. Quagmire to arrive. The only noise was that of the crickets chirping in the night. Jonah wanted desperately to break the silence and say something to Angie. But he didn't dare say a word with Edgar frowning bitterly in the seat next to him. So, Jonah tried to make eye

88

contact with her. He looked at her through the rear view mirror. But Angie sat in the backseat staring out the passenger window, oblivious to Jonah's gaze.

As 11:30 approached Edgar opened the glove box and handed the men nylon stockings and gloves. Shem, Jonah and Edgar pulled the stockings down over their heads and put on their gloves. The kidnappers and Angie sat in the car waiting for Dr. Quagmire. All was quiet.

Suddenly, the kidnappers heard music playing from somewhere. It was coming from somewhere near Mutt's Meteor.

"What is that?" Jonah whispered.

"Music," Edgar whispered back.

"I know that, but where is it coming from?"

Edgar didn't seem too concerned, "Probably some kids in the park with a radio."

Jonah strained to listen to the music. It was faint, barely audible.

"It's a Beach..." before Jonah could say anything else a strange sort of creature jumped out from the night. It appeared to be a bird flapping enormous black wings. Jonah quickly turned on the headlights. The strange animal was gone.

"What was that?" Jonah asked.

Edgar pulled out his gun muttering to himself, "Stupid bastard Quagmire always playing games. Relax Palace or Pain Palace? You stupid..."

Suddenly, there was a loud stomp from the back of the car. Angie screamed. Jonah screamed. Edgar turned towards the direction of the noise prepared to shoot. Shem covered his ears. Now the stomping was coming from the top of the car.

"It's on the roof," shouted Edgar. He opened his door and stepped out. The strange creature jumped onto the hood of the car and the kidnappers and Angie saw that it was in fact a man. A man dressed in black with a cape. He stood in the headlights and danced to the Beach Boys' *Sloop John B* and then flapped his arms like a bird and ran off laughing.

Edgar got back into the car, turned towards Angie and said, "Looks like Daddy has a profound understanding of the absurd. First, he decides to pay us $3,253 and tonight wants to entertain us with this…freak show."

Although the kidnappers and Angie were still a bit shaken by the stranger, they tried to remain calm. But as the hour approached midnight, and there was still no sign of Dr. Quagmire, Angie began to cry. She couldn't understand what was going on or why her father simply couldn't pay the kidnappers. "What's wrong with my father," she moaned.

Off in the distance, about 50 feet from the car, a faint figure approached. "Edgar, look," said Jonah pointing towards Mutt's Meteor.

Edgar stepped out of the car and squinted in the direction of advancing figure. "Dr. Quagmire," Edgar whispered to himself. Dr. Quagmire stood, about twenty feet from the car, carrying a large black case.

Edgar yelled to Dr. Quagmire, "Quagmire, just put the case with the money on the ground and turn around. Once we have the money the girl goes free."

"No way!" Dr. Quagmire shouted back. "First Angie goes free then I'll give you the money."

"This is not a negotiation you idiot," yelled Edgar turning red

90

in the face.

"How do I know you have Angie?" asked Dr. Quagmire.

Edgar turned on the interior light of the car and Jonah turned off the headlights. Dr. Quagmire saw his daughter in the backseat.

Dr. Quagmire said nothing else. He put the case with the money down and turned his back to the kidnappers. Edgar motioned to Jonah to get the money. Jonah ran and took the case and ran back to the car with it. He gave the case to Shem.

Shem counted the money and then recounted the money. Edgar was watching his old friend as he counted. Shem looked up and shook his head and then made the following series of hand gestures to Edgar – three – two – five – three. Edgar thought for a moment and then shouted out at Dr. Quagmire, "You're short $3,253 Quagmire."

"Well, you said you got paid $3,253, so I figured I could deduct the…"

"You cheap bastard…" howled Edgar. He was so angry with Dr. Quagmire that he couldn't even speak; he simply stood there sputtering and fuming, shaking his fists in the air.

Edgar refused to let the doctor off without paying the full sum of $500,000. He refused to let the doctor win. "Quagmire, I want whatever jewelry you are wearing…Your watch, your wedding ring. And I want your wallet. Put these things on the ground in front of you."

Dr. Quagmire did as he was told and turned his back to the kidnappers. Jonah ran and fetched the items and brought them to Edgar so he could examine them. Edgar couldn't believe his eyes. The doctor had a simple gold band for a wedding ring, a Swatch, and his wallet had $40 in cash and a couple of credit cards.

Edgar pounded the roof of the car feebly. Enough was enough.

He just wanted to end this fiasco he had started. He handed the items to Shem and then growled, "Let the girl go free."

Jonah, reluctantly, painfully opened the passenger door. He offered his hand to Angie but she refused Jonah's help and pulled herself out on her own. She took a deep breath and began the 20 foot journey back to her father. After taking a couple of steps Jonah yelled out, "Wait."

"What now?" complained Edgar jumping up and down enraged.

Jonah walked past Angie and approached Dr. Quagmire. "Sir, I know this is unorthodox," Jonah was nervous and his voice wavered a bit, "but I want to ask for your daughter's hand in marriage."

"You've got to be kidding?" Dr. Quagmire shrieked through clenched teeth "You kidnapped her you little putrid piece of crap."

"I know that sir, but I'm not really a kidnapper." Jonah turned towards Angie, pulled the stocking off of his head, and began to address her. "I'm a small time thief, a con, cheat but not a kidnapper. But I don't regret that I kidnapped you, Angie." Jonah thought that this last line was a very romantic thing to say.

"I'm getting the hell out of here," Edgar muttered to himself as he walked round the car to the driver's side. Shem was already in the backseat clutching the case of money.

"Angie sweetheart, don't pay any attention to this bum," said Dr. Quagmire walking towards Angie. Jonah, though, stepped in front of him and pulled out a gun. "I hate to have to do this sir, but I can't let you go any further. You need to calm down so we can talk about this rationally," Jonah instructed his prospective father-in-law. The doctor stopped in his tracks and howled, "SHADE."

Jimmy Shade suddenly jumped out from behind a bush about

30 feet from the kidnapper's car. "Looks like I picked out the perfect piece of music for this little get together," he announced smugly. He then pressed a button on his RCM3 and the Beatles' *Baby in Black* began to play.

Edgar fired at Jimmy Shade. He shot a tree about twenty feet from Jimmy Shade but the gunshot scared Jimmy Shade, and he dropped the RCM3. It fell to the ground and broke into pieces. The machine laid there lifeless.

"You killed the Beatles you…you…Nazi," screamed Jimmy Shade. He pulled out his ruby handled, silver plated, lone ranger style shootout, special edition pistol.

"Who's he Quagmire, your illegitimate son?" quipped Edgar.

"You Beatle killing fascist. Take that." Jimmy Shade fired the first of what would be about a near infinite amount of errant bullets. This one zipped over the head of Edgar past Dr. Quagmire and into a wooded area near the boulder, past a maple and into the left shoulder of Martha Frigs who was watching this drama unfold from a tree. The bullet ripped through her arm and she fell from the tree and hit the ground with a thud. Her last thought before she lost consciousness was how much she would enjoy watching the hit men drown her ex-husband in a pool of creamed corn and applesauce.

"Shoot *him*," screamed Dr. Quagmire pointing at Jonah. Soon the errant bullets seemed to be flying from all directions. The whole of Mutt's Meteor popped, hissed, boomed and banged like a 4th of July celebration. Jonah, Angie and Dr. Quagmire fell to the ground and laid on their stomachs.

Dr. Quagmire began to slither his way towards his daughter. "Angie," he shouted, "don't be fooled by your emotions. It is perfectly natural for a captive to feel emotions of loyalty or sympathy towards their captor. It's happened to lots of people before. It's called the Stockholm Syndrome. Remember…"

"Angie. I love you," yelled Jonah. Angie laid there looking at Jonah. "I LOVE YOU," Jonah repeated.

"You do not love her you stupid son of a…" Dr. Quagmire launched himself on top of Jonah and began to wrestle with him for the gun.

"Sir, I will not fight you…seeing as you are going to be my father-in-law," said Jonah curling himself into the fetal position. Dr. Quagmire stood up and began kicking Jonah.

"I'm going to kill you," screamed Dr. Quagmire. "AAAAAAAHHHHHHHH." His kicks became more furious and violent.

Suddenly, the good doctor went limp and fell to the ground like a building collapsing underneath its demolition.

"Oh, my god," panicked Angie crawling over to him, "Oh, my god." She frantically looked for where her father had been shot. She turned him this way and that, examining his clothes. Looking for blood. But there was none. Jonah sat up painfully and saw Shem standing in the headlights. He had the case of money tucked under one arm and he was holding the doctors watch, ring and wallet in his hands. His eyes were closed and he was chanting.

Edgar believed he had Jimmy Shade in his sights. He fired and hit another tree but Shade fell to the ground with a thud. He laid on his back and sang out the refrain to *Help!* in defiance of death. He died in mid refrain.

The guns were silent. Edgar cautiously stood up and barked out, "Let's get the hell out of here." But before anyone had a chance to move a muscle, two enormous hulking brutes strode out from the

94

shadows. Both were tall, no-necked monsters. Their guns smoking in their hands. They walked in unison, and they stepped over the body of Jimmy Shade and proceeded to the scene of the drop-off.

Brute number 1 addressed the group, "OK, boys and girls let's put the guns down." The man's voice was thick and bloody like a raw steak.

"Who the hell are you?" asked Edgar throwing his gun to the ground. Jonah dropped his weapon as well. The quiet brute collected them from the ground.

"The question is who the hell are you? Specifically, which one of you is Ron Frigs." Everyone was silent. They could hear police sirens shrieking from far away.

"Listen people, we don't have a lot of time before the cops get here. Lets, make this simple. We have a nice gift we need to give Ron Frigs..."

"Yeah, we want to take him out for a bite to eat," giggled brute number 2.

"So, again, which one of you is Ron Frigs?" Again there was silence.

Edgar then pointed in the direction of Dr. Quagmire and said, "He is."

Angie immediately protested, "He is not. He's my father."

Then Shem whistled to get the men's attention. Both men turned towards Shem who still held the doctor's personal items and the case of money in his hands. Shem pointed in the direction of Jimmy Shade.

Brute number 1 complained, "But I shot him. He's dead." Both men strode over to Jimmy Shade dejectedly like little boys being forced to come to the dinner table when they would rather be playing outside.

"Check him for ID," the one brute said to the other.

Brute number 2 gave cursory check of Jimmy Shade and announced, "Where? The guy is wearing tights and a cape. He doesn't have any pockets."

"Mrs. Frigs said he was a freak."

"He sure is a freak."

And with that, brute number 2 picked up Jimmy Shade and they were about to march off into the woods when brute number 1 walked back over to Shem.

"Thanks pop," he said with mock affection. He patted Shem's cheek and then pulled at the case of money Shem held in his arms. Shem tried to resist and the man struggled a bit, but the case popped out of Shem's arms like a cork from a champagne bottle. Both men disappeared into the woods as mysteriously as they had appeared.

As Edgar watched the two men march off with *his* money, he became furious and he began to scream at Jonah, "This is all your fault. You screwed this whole thing up. All you had to do is let the girl go free, but instead…you ruined everything. Everything." Edgar wished he had his gun so he could shoot Jonah.

"$500,000, kid…it was ours…and you pissed it down the drain with that stupid punk stunt. You want to marry her? Well, you better hurry." Edgar was alluding to the fact that cops were getting closer and closer. He climbed into the driver's seat and called out, "Shem get in."

Shem looked over at Jonah. Jonah stood forlornly, his eyes downcast, staring at the ground. As Shem was still shutting the door, the car sped down the footpath and out of the park. In seconds it was gone.

Jonah and Angie stood in the park as an avalanche of sirens

96

was fast approaching. Jonah was motionless. "Well, you better run," Angie said. But he remained motionless.

She walked over to where he stood and she lifted his face so that their eyes met. She didn't need to speak. Jonah could see what he believed to be urgency on her face. She's worried about me, he thought. He looked deep into her sparkling eyes and without a second thought he kissed her.

This was not a kiss of the magnitude of exploding fireworks or flashes of lightning and booming thunder. This was not a kiss of euphoria and epiphany. Instead, this was an awkward kiss shared by two people, one a little nervous and the other a little fearful, in the pitch darkness while sirens howled and moaned in the night. Angie instinctively pulled herself away. "What was that?" she asked.

Jonah was confused, and then a smile bloomed on his face.

He began to run in the direction of the wooded area. He yelled to Angie over his shoulder, "Angie, I'll meet you at Fool Runs Creek at 11:30."

As he disappeared from sight Angie shook her head and thought, "11:30 in the morning or in the evening?"

The End

As Jimmy Shade died he saw his life, from birth to death, zip past like a speeding car. He felt overwhelmed by a flood of emotion. He felt as though he was naked and raw, and he could taste something like salt in his mouth. A voice then unearthed itself from the center of his mind, like some long sleeping colossus ripping itself free from the earth, debris falling from its words. "So what do you think?" the voice asked.

Jimmy Shade was then absorbed in light and he saw that his

leotards had turned white and his cape was silver. In his hand was his resurrected RCM3 device. "This is what I think," he said as he pushed the play button.

The Beach Boys' *Let's Go Away for Awhile* began to play, and as the song played Jimmy Shade was now back at the park where he had been killed. He felt as if he was getting lighter. He started to float away. Just before the last traces of his consciousness evaporated, he saw the playing field of human emotion beneath him. He saw the hit men loading his body into the trunk of a car. He saw Martha Frigs, fallen to the earth and unconscious. He saw Jonah at the edge of a wooded area watching Angie from the distance. He saw hundreds of policemen running, with weapons drawn, towards Mutt's Meteor. There, near the meteor stood Angie. Dr. Quagmire was sprawled out at her feet, fast asleep and snoring, and then, pop, Jimmy Shade was gone.

Doomsday Garden Party

J oe Lillywhite lived a desperately quiet existence, and he found the complete and utter silence that devoured him day and night unbearable. In order to obliterate the silence, he had filled his apartment with noise making machines. He bought televisions, stereos, portable radios, anything that could erase the quiet with the touch of a button. But these machines simply spoke at you. Dialog simply didn't exist, and Joe wanted conversation. Since meaningful relationships with other humans, whether virtual or real, ranged from emotionally tricky to physically confounding for Joe, he decided to buy a *do-it-yourself* speaking-robot kit.

When the post office delivered the 5 cardboard boxes, varying in size from slightly enormous to minuscule, containing the bits and pieces of the robot, Joe decided then and there that his robot must have a name. So, he began to create a mental list of names, and for some reason the familiar, yet strangely foreign name, *Fred Deller* stood out from the others. He shall be called Fred, Joe thought.

Joe then spent the next five months trying to assemble Fred. He toiled and struggled to give Fred life. Unfortunately for the robot (and Joe for that matter), Joe reached a stage in the construction process where he realized that he had made a vital mistake in one of the first steps and the only way to fix the mistake required dismantling Fred and beginning again. Being faced with the reality that he had to deconstruct and then reconstruct his partially built co-communicator, Joe decided to quietly surrender. He parked Fred in the living room next to the television, and from there Fred surveyed the room sightlessly, a symbol of the bleak and unbreakable silence consuming Joe.

Since Fred had failed to save him from the eternal quiet of his life, Joe formulated plan B: work. He dedicated himself to his job the way a monk dedicates himself to his God. Body and soul. Eight years of long, hard work later, Joe was arguably considered one of the best FBI Agents working for the Department of Disinformation, or DoDis for short. The other agents of DoDis even referred to the Baltimore Field Office where Joe worked as *Joe's place*, acknowledging the fact that Joe seemed to live there.

The Ancient Art of Thought Clogging

In the intelligence business, the classic pattern for hiding what the government termed Surreptitious Infractions of Necessity, or SIN, was the "cover up." But this pattern was reactive by nature, tended to be messy, prone to human error and vulnerable to investigation. It always seemed that no matter how stealthily the powerful tried to

100

sweep damning evidence under the carpet, the investigators always looked there first.   The problem with the cover up pattern presented itself clearly to the Supervising Agents of DoDis: investigators. If the investigators did not investigate, then the government, and *the institution*s aligned with the government, could operate freely and without the annoying threat of being caught in a SIN. This led to the invention of a new pattern to conceal SINs that was actually not new at all and had been practiced by juntas and psychopath megalomaniacs throughout history all over the world: Thought Clogging, or Tc for short. No one had stated the first law of Tc as succinctly and as poetically as Flash Boing, the unofficial guru of Tc. Boing had once said

> Make sure that people's minds
> Are full of wet sloppy shit,
> Then you can do whatever you want
> And get away with it.

Tc promised the men and women in power that they wouldn't have to worry about messy cover ups anymore. In todays world, the powerful would be able to commit whatever sort of SIN they wanted and the masses, as well as bothersome investigators, would be too distracted, too Tced, to really understand what was in fact happening.

Flash Boing had trained Joe and the other agents of DoDis in the ancient art of Tc, and on their graduation day they recited the following oath

I [place your name here] promise to do my best to make sure that the people of [your country of origin] will remain healthily disinformed and Tced so that our leaders will be free to commit any SIN they want without the anxiety of being caught.

Just Beyond the Enigma Cypher Chip

Throughout the halls of DoDis, the history of the department's impact on the ideological framework of everyday American life was on display. Technological innovations developed in DoDis's laboratories sat under the domes and cubes of glass display cases. Documents, resting on podiums or framed and hanging from the walls, attested to the influence of DoDis throughout history. Gold plated plaques acknowledged the dedication and hard work of exemplary agents.

Just beyond the Enigma Cypher Chip display was an open space that Joe believed was left vacant for him. Joe knew that every agent of DoDis understood how valuable he was and how important his service was to the department. Joe had developed into a true expert in Tc.

His greatest Tc achievement was a website he had created in order to distract attention from a scandal that involved a certain Senator who was pulled over by the police for reckless driving. The Senator was not only drunk, he was driving naked, a bottle of vodka between his legs, and an inflatable poodle was buckled into the passenger seat of his car.

Now this particular Senator was the younger brother of the President, and the President expressed that he didn't want to see his baby brother portrayed by the press as a drunken pervert. In order to rescue the Senator from the frying pan and the fire, the Agents of DoDis injected a series of Tc stories into mainstream media. Their mandate was to bury the story of the Senator: *Codename Rapunzel*.

Joe's contribution to *Rapunzel* was a website that was a work of Tc artistry like nothing ever seen before. It was subtly deceptive, uncannily believable and pure fabrication. The website published an "alien manual recovered from the Roswell crash site from 1947."

DoDis had been trying to manipulate public opinion ever since Roswell first became a happening. The latest tactic was not to try to debunk those that believed it, but to pose as believers and say the most extraordinarily preposterous things. Joe's website did exactly this.

The manual, according to the website, "was translated into English by a couple of aliens that had survived the crash and that now reside somewhere in the US. No one knows where, though." The manual was titled *The Official Field Guide of the Universe,* or TOFGU for short.

Joe took great pride in this website and the disinformation that it contained and the fact that the site did exactly what it was intended to do. Great numbers of Americans frequented the site and had their thoughts clogged by it daily. A great many debated the authenticity of the information it contained, and a great many believed that the information was authentic and were deeply concerned with the way the TOFGU defined earthlings. According to the manual, "Earthling's are variety of earth mammal that have the ability to speak."

"So this is what the residents of the universe think of earthlings? We are merely animals that can speak?" was the typical question posted on the forum dedicated to discussing the TOFGU. This revelation shocked almost everyone that read the TOFGU because they immediately assumed that other life forms throughout the universe would probably treat us as badly as we treat earth mammals.

So, while people privately and publicly debated the TOFGU, or whether the residents of the universe saw us as animals and were going to eventually arrive to turn us into steaks or grind us up into hamburger meat, people were less concerned with the fact that Senators were driving around drunk and naked with inflatable poodles.

Turn on the War

One humid, gray summer morning in Baltimore, Herb Schmeltz, the Supervising Agent of DoDis, called Joe to his office in order to discuss a serious threat to the security of the American people. Joe arrived promptly. Schmeltz's receptionist was busy on the phone. She whispered to Joe, placing her hand over the phone's mouthpiece, "He's expecting you." The door to Schmeltz's office was closed. A silver plated placard hung from the door which stated the fifth law of Tc:

> You may forget the first four laws
> But try hard to remember this -
> As the warheads corkscrew through the sky
> Make sure that all believe
> War is not mass violence
> It's just a Doomsday Garden Party.

Before Joe entered, he stood for a moment and collected himself. He was among the select few that had ever been invited into the confines of Schmeltz's office. He adjusted his tie, took a deep breath and opened the door. Inside the office the shades were drawn and the lights were off. It was as dark as a crypt with the exception of a computer monitor that threw its light like a spotlight on Schmeltz's broad red face. Schmeltz's assistant, Agent Dewey Longburger, sat at his side, only partially visible.

Joe closed the door and began to feel his way through the darkness. With arms outstretched in front of him, Joe slowly navigated the pitch darkness, feeling his way to Schmeltz's desk.

When Joe finally reached the desk and sat down, Schmeltz began, "Joe, I'm ashamed to admit this but the state of secrecy that we protect has been breached. I am not sure how it has happened or who is responsible. But I am sure that a piece, a fragment if you will, of the intelligence that is our duty to keep secret and hide from the

104

surveillance of others has been sold to a writer of fiction."

Longburger elaborated, "Joe, it seems that someone by the name of James Alexander Shade has written a book that set off a few alarms in the bureau. This book of his, *The Mass Extinction Event*, seems to contain some information that...well...is classified. Top Secret stuff." Longburger slid a large book, a book as thick as the Bible, to Joe. Joe picked it up and began to thumb through the pages.

"Now strangely enough Shade is dead. Someone murdered him two weeks ago. The police found Shade's body in a bathtub that was filled with creamed corn and applesauce. He had also been shot for good measure. It appears that the gunshot was the cause of death and that the applesauce and creamed corn was simply some sicko's idea of theater." Longburger paused to allow Joe to examine the *The Mass Extinction Event* but because the lighting was so poor he couldn't make out a word, not even the title of the book.

Schmeltz leaned forward and asked quietly, "Ever hear of Project Dead Duck, Joe?" Joe shook his head looking up from the book. Schmeltz's face shone like the giant Red Spot on Jupiter and Longburger's glasses fiendishly reflected the light from the monitor.

"Not long ago," Longburger continued, "the President met with his chief advisers, the heads of the Department of Defense, and some big name Hollywood producers in order to investigate the possibility of turning war into a reality style TV program. The President wanted to turn the next war the US would wage into a game show of sorts. Think *Survivor* Joe. People would be recruited to fight on teams and their participation would be aired on national television. Hollywood wanted to advertise it with the slogan *Turn on the War*. The trouble is that James Alexander Shade published this exact same scenario in *that* book." He pointed to the book Joe held in his hands. "But it gets worse. We are now seeing websites springing up that are publishing some excerpts from Shade's book. Believe it or not, people are reading that...that...crap and taking it seriously."

"People, as you know Joe, are capable of believing the most ridiculous things. There is a group of conspirators that believe this type of thing that Shade is talking about is actually in the works," Schmletz laughed. It seemed that he couldn't believe that people were actually capable of believing something so ridiculous was possible, even though it was clearly possible.

There was a pause in the conversation at this point. All three men sat silently. Joe sat quietly wondering what they wanted him to do. Schmeltz and Longburger sat and intently watched Joe.

"Take a look at this site Joe," Schmeltz rotated his monitor towards him. Joe craned his neck to get a better look at what Schmeltz wanted him to see. He saw a simple web page that had some quoted text. He began to read a passage but Schmeltz redirected his attention to a Hyperlink at the bottom of a page that read, "Ever heard of the dead duck project?"

"The link is dead," said Schmeltz as he clicked the link and an error page opened. "But as you can see, we have every right to be concerned. The state of secrecy that we preserve and maintain has been violated. The web master of this site may even have a complete copy of the Project Dead Duck file."

"It appears that a file is missing from Senator Weezel's office," admitted Longburger. "We believe that the man that operates this site has this file. We also suspect that he was involved in the murder of Shade."

"What do you want me to do, sir?" Joe asked Schmeltz.

Schmeltz leaned back in his chair, "Well, I'm giving you

clearance for protocol N0-T4U-2C."

Joe had never heard of such a protocol. He reasoned that it must be something extremely top-secret, and of course in the intelligence game secrecy directly correlated to value. The more secret the piece of intelligence, then the more valuable. Joe felt strangely honored. His hard work at the bureau was finally paying off.

Schmeltz slid a manila folder to Joe. He picked up the file from the desk and opened it. Joe could clearly make out the title on the cover sheet, "PROTOCOL N0-T4U-2C." He flipped to the first page but again, because of the poor lighting he could barely make out a word.

"We have made contact with the web master of the site you just saw. His online name is ObiWan," stated Longburger. "His real name is Fred Bower."

Schmeltz interrupted, "We want you to act as agent provocateur, Joe. Your assignment in simple. Find out if he has the file. If he has it, we'll determine what to do next."

"You'll meet this Fred Bower character tomorrow at 12:00 noon..." Longburger handed Joe a photo of Fred Bower. The photo reflected the light from the monitor and Joe saw that it was terribly out of focus. Bower's face was a featureless smudge. Joe was about to ask if they had a better photo but Schmeltz didn't give him a chance. "The meeting place is room 15 in the Rex Hotel in Ersatz Michigan. The same room where Shade's body was found. We've reserved it for you."

"Your flight leaves tonight at 7 pm," Agent Longburger handed Joe an envelope containing the airline ticket. "Good luck Joe." Longburger shook Joe's hand.

"Oh, I almost forgot, Bower is meeting with you because he is interested in video footage of two senators discussing Project Dead

107

Duck." Longburger handed Joe a DVD and smiled dully.

"Remember Joe, if you succeed, we succeed," said Schmeltz with a wink.

Subversive Agents Everywhere

Before leaving for Ersatz, Joe did a little research on the Protocol N0-T4U-2C. According to the records in the FBI archive, the protocol was written in 1947 by a paranoid Agent named Arthur K. Rover. Rover was desperately afraid that Russian agents had infiltrated the US and were trying to undermine the Government by systematically and strategically instilling panic and fear in ordinary citizens. In 1947, Rover watched as the number of UFO sightings exploded. It seemed that everyone was seeing flying saucers and little green Martians. He realized that something needed to be done. What exactly? Well, those Russian Commie spies that were reporting all these UFOs needed to be exposed. If they couldn't be exposed as Russian spies, they needed to be exposed as frauds, liars, cheats, traitors, and/or perverts. So protocol N0-T4U-2C was born. It was given the working title "HOW TO NEUTRALIZE SUBVERSIVE AGENTS IN 5 EASY STEPS" and began with the melodramatic and overtly paranoid warning, "SUBVERSIVE AGENTS ARE EVERYWHERE."

Shortly after drafting the procedure, Agent Rover seemed to lose grip of reality. He filed an official complaint to his Supervising Agent claiming that Russian spies had drafted the procedure and planted it in his office. He also started showing up to work with his poodle, Spencer, whom he claimed was Benjamin Franklin reincarnated. According to Agent Rover, Spencer wanted him to redraft the Declaration of Independence to include the statement that

108

all men are entitled to "...Life, Liberty, the pursuit of Happiness and the freedom to hump the mailman's legs." He was duly removed from duty and never heard of again.

Flying the Friendly Skies

As the plane prepared for take off from the Baltimore Airport and as travelers filed into the plane searching for luggage space and their seats, Joe sat in his window seat reading over protocol N0-T4U-2C. He had studied the protocol all day long and was still having a difficult time determining how to best implement it. He found it vague and confusing. He was also having a difficult time understanding how following the protocol would actually accomplish what it proclaimed it could, namely "neutralizing a subversive agent."

As soon as he would come across what he considered to be a sound plan of action, the plan would either evaporate, spring a leak, implode or simply fall to pieces. He shoved the protocol back into his briefcase with a sigh, placed his briefcase under his seat and closed his eyes. He needed to clear his mind. So, he resigned himself to resting for the flight.

The moment his eyes closed, an enormous man collapsed into the seat next to Joe. He had apparently just devoured a plate or two of pasta. His shirt wore the telltale tomato stains, and he stank of garlic. As he painfully squeezed himself into the seat, excess flesh spilled over into Joe's area. Joe tried hard to pull himself away from the invading flab and he peevishly turned towards the window. After making himself comfortable, Joe closed his eyes and fell asleep.

Joe had been asleep for half an hour when the sound of someone yelling, dragged him from his slumber. "Mr. Filbert, don't worry we'll have you out in no time," a flight attendant was screaming from somewhere. Joe opened his eyes. He drowsily looked around to see where the commotion was coming from. At the rear of the plane, a group of flight attendants had gathered outside of one of the four tiny bathrooms that existed on the flight. While some of them half heartedly examined the bathroom door, an attendant named Janet was yelling out to Mr. Filbert, "Sir, we'll have you out in no time." Although she yelled out such statements, her face was clouded with doubt. She knew she was lying.

An old lady with white hair and unhappy eyes, sitting in front of Joe, peered over the back of her seat and complained, "That man flying with you has been stuck in the toilet since we took off." Joe suddenly realized that the seat next to his was in fact vacant.

"He isn't traveling with me, he's just sitting next to me." Joe said yawning and picking up a magazine that was laying in Mr. Filbert's vacant seat.

"All I can say is, thank God there's more than one toilet on this bucket," she muttered back.

The flight attendant that had been yelling to Mr. Filbert hurried over to the aisle of seats where Joe sat, and she addressed him with sugar-sweet politeness, "Sir, we are going to need your help to try to free your travel companion from the toilet."

"He *isn't* my travel companion," said Joe looking over the top of the magazine, turning the page. "He is just some fat guy sitting next to me."

"Well, he's stuck....and..." A bell rang. Joe and the flight attendant looked up and saw that the fasten seat-belt sign had been lit. The attendant said, "Hmmph," as she left Joe and briskly walked to the front of the airplane.

She sweetly announced into the intercom, "The ride might get a little bumpy from here on out, ladies and gentlemen. So, please return to your seats and make sure your seat belts are securely fastened. Thank you."

As she walked back down the aisle towards the bathroom, she stopped at Joe's row of seats and said irritably, "Sir, could you at least help us try to extract your neighbor from the toilet? It seems..." The airplane suddenly bounced. She staggered for a moment and then regained her balance. Seeing a line of people waiting at the other toilet, she yelled out, "Please return to your seats." She turned on Joe savagely, "Will you help us or not?"

"What about the fasten seat belt sign?" Joe protested meekly. But the flight attendant was impassive. She stood with her arms folded against her chest, tapping her foot impatiently.

Joe, finding this whole affair depressing, sighed and asked bitterly, "What do you want me to do?"

Joe followed the attendant to the toilet. "Please explain to him that we are doing our best and we will have him out as soon as possible."

Joe knocked on the door and Mr. Filbert screamed out, "Get me the hell out of here."

"What's his name?" Joe asked the flight attendant.

"Mr. Filbert."

"Mr. Filbert, the airplane staff are all working very hard to get you out of the bathroom. So, just sit tight and you'll be out in no time." Joe tried hard to sound chipper.

"Sit tight?" howled Mr. Filbert. "What the hell do you think I'm doing jerky? Who the hell are you?"

"The guy that has the seat next to you."

"Yeah, well I want to talk to the pilot. Not some asshole

passenger..."

"Well, the pilot is a little busy flying the plane right now," Joe shot back sarcastically. He didn't like being called an *asshole* by anyone. But he especially took offense when someone as grotesquely overweight as Mr. Filbert called him an *asshole*.

"Yeah right. He can't put the plane on autopilot? What about the co-pilot? Is he stuck in the other bathroom?"

Joe couldn't resist the opportunity that Mr. Filbert had just handed him, "No. The copilot isn't stuck in the other bathroom because he isn't the size of a walrus like you...you tubby moron," he yelled back.

"Wait until I get out of here," screamed Mr. Filbert. He began to grunt and groan and howl. He kicked at the bathroom door like a mule kicking in its stall. Joe backed away from the door, a bit frightened by the sudden violence brewing inside the bathroom,

He was about to insult Mr. Filbert again when the flight attendant interrupted Joe and said, "OK, that's enough." She was irritated and her face was crumpled into a dissatisfied frown. "Please return to your seat," she instructed Joe pointing in the direction of his seat.

"Listen, you asked me to help..." Joe protested loudly as he sat down.

For the rest of the flight Joe's plump neighbor was stuck in the bathroom. The flight attendants had given up their mission of solace and had informed him that he was just going to have to wait until the plane landed.

So, as the plane flew the friendly skies from Baltimore to Detroit, Mr. Filbert screamed and howled, "Get me the hell out of here, you idiots." Which was usually followed by a series of violent kicks to

112

the bathroom door.

By the time the plane landed everyone was weary from the constant bellowing of Mr. Filbert. As the plane rolled to a stop, everyone simultaneously jumped from their seats. Those that had luggage stored in the overhead luggage compartments rudely pushed and pulled people out of their way in order to gain access to their luggage. People were cursing each other under their breath. It was an explosively sensitive situation. Mr. Filbert was still screaming but the nature of his screams had changed from impolite pleas for help to threats. "Wait until I get a hold of my lawyer," he yelled.

As the passengers waited impatiently to exit, two mechanics with grease stained uniforms and baseball caps boarded the plane. They tried to politely part the sea of travelers, trying to navigate their way to the bathroom that held Mr. Filbert captive. But the passengers were in no mood to be pushed around by people working for the airline after an hour and a half of sheer torture. They pushed back. Soon pushes became punches. People were screaming. The mechanics yelled for help, drowning in a sea of irate travelers. The old woman with the gray hair and unhappy eyes, swinging her purse whacking people indiscriminately, sounded the battle cry, "Lets kill these loony bastards." The passengers stampeded, trampling those that had fallen underfoot in order to disembark.

Joe was one of the lucky ones that didn't fall in the violent exodus. He casually walked from the wave of violence that had spilled out into the waiting area at the gate and proceeded to the Avatar car rental office where a car had been reserved for him. He scribbled his signature on a rental agreement form, grabbed the keys and was off.

Room Number 15 in the Rex Hotel

By the time Joe reached the Rex Hotel it was 10:00 at night. He found the hotel easily. It was situated on Main Street between Trojan Dry Cleaners and the Greasy Burger Diner. The Rex Hotel had seen better years, presumably. What Joe saw was a building with one foot in the grave. In the streetlight, he saw that whatever color it had been painted when it was first constructed had given way to the color of goose liver paté. The entrance to the hotel was a glass door that had been shattered in multiple places. In an attempt to repair the door, someone had placed pieces of duct tape here and there to keep the shattered glass intact. The illuminated sign that at one time proudly announced 'Rex Hotel' now flickered dimly 'R ot'. Joe parked his car in the street and sat spellbound. He told himself, "So this is where Shade was murdered."

Joe entered the hotel and quickly realized that there was no front office. Instead, there was a bar. Seated at the bar were eight or nine chain smoking bar flies. All heads turned towards Joe as he entered. He was simultaneously inspected by the glassy eyes of drunks that were driving full throttle down the highway of inebriation. From the jukebox bounced the quirky and spirited Dusty Springfield song, *Stay Awhile*. Joe walked up to the bar and said to the bartender, "Who do I see about a room?"

The bartender was an old hunchback of a man, grizzled with age. He seemed to have difficulty standing upright and he grimaced and winced with pain. He was concentrating on pouring a shot of whiskey when Joe asked about a room. Doing his best to ignore Joe, he overfilled the glass and the excess whiskey spilled on the countertop. Satisfied, he pushed the shot glass in the direction of a customer. The bartender looked Joe in the eye. He staggered a bit.

114

Squinted. "So, you're the jackass that wants a room for the night?"

Joe shrugged his shoulders and nodded his head as if to say, "Yeah, so?"

"I usually rent rooms by the hour, if you know what I mean," frowned the bartender.

Joe said nothing. He stood silently with his mouth agape. The bartender handed Joe a key, "Top of the stairs, on the left. Number 15."

Looking around and seeing no sign of stairs, Joe asked, "Where are the stairs?"

"Behind the curtain," grumbled the bartender impatiently.

To the right of the bar hung a red velvet curtain the size of a normal doorway. Joe pushed the curtain aside and saw before him a wooden staircase that had been put together by a blind man. The steps were uneven and slanted up and down. The wood of some of the steps had rotted to a point that the step was patched together with other smaller bits of ill fitting wood. As Joe climbed the stairs he heard the bartender and his patrons laughing. He knew they were joking about him.

The stairs ended, and Joe found himself in a hallway that groaned and creaked under his every step. Most of the hall lights had burned out, and the couple lights that still functioned, flickered every now and again signaling their imminent demise. Joe passed room number 11, number 13, and then came to a room that didn't have door. He dropped his briefcase in disbelief. He walked to the next room and saw that it was numbered 17. It isn't possible, he thought. He picked up his briefcase and walked back down to the bar.

"Excuse me," he said to the bartender, who was again sloppily pouring another shot of whiskey. "It seems that my room is missing its door."

The bartender said without looking up, "The police kicked it in."

"Could I get a different room for the night?"

The bartender, looking up at Joe but still pouring whiskey into the shot glass and onto the countertop, remarked, "I'm sorry, but all the other rooms have been booked weeks in advance." The bar erupted into a chorus of cackles. A couple of old drunks at the bar were laughing so hard that they fell out of their seats. An old toothless man dressed in clothes that were two sizes too large for him shouted, "Yeah, this is a real vacation hot spot."

Joe allowed for the squall of laughter to subside and then asked, "Well, can you put a door on my room?"

Again, the bar exploded with laughter. One of the drunks that had fallen off his chair was laughing so hard that he wet his pants. He stood in a puddle wiping tears from his eyes. Joe realized that help was not forthcoming. So, he walked away defeated, pulled the curtain aside and rambled up the surrealistic staircase to his room.

Joe, the Rat and Mitsy

Standing outside his room, Joe peered into its depth like someone would peer into a murky pool of water looking for signs of animal or insect life. He had the strange feeling that someone or something occupied the room. He stepped inside cautiously and flipped on the lights. The lights illuminated laboriously, and some cockroaches scurried across the yellow linoleum floor and disappeared under the bed. The room was dirty, dingy, damp and smelled like an ashtray. In the center of the room, with it's headboard against the wall, was the bed. At the foot of the bed was a small wooden stool.

116

Hanging on the wall, just above the headboard of the bed, was a coin operated telephone.

There was another door which was closed. Joe assumed it was the bathroom. He jerked the door open and turned on the lights. The room stank of raw sewage and standing water. There was a pile of clothes in the corner of the room. The rotten smell was overpowering. Joe put his hand over his mouth and nose and ventured inside. He bent over to examine the items in the corner of the room when an enormous rat pounced out of the refuse and squealed viciously at him. Joe scrambled from the room and slammed the door close. The rat banged itself against the door making loud thuds. "Sweet Jesus..." exclaimed Joe as he held the door firmly closed.

Joe pushed the door closed and pressed against it with all of his weight. He wasn't about to let the creature out of the bathroom. It continued to bang and squeal and hiss from inside the bathroom. Suddenly, a hand reached out and touched Joe's shoulder. Joe screamed and slapped at the hand on his shoulder thinking it was another rat. He turned around screaming and saw standing before him the oddest sight he had ever seen in his life.

"Who the hell are you?" asked Joe still pushing against the door. The rat was still beating itself against the door and the hollow thuds echoed in the hallway.

"I'm Mitsy," she said with a voice that had been worn down by a lifetime of cigarettes and whiskey.

There were many odd things about Mitsy, but the most obvious was her handlebar mustache. Now, Mitsy was not young by any stretch of the imagination, but she had put great effort into hiding her age behind a veil of makeup. In the pursuit of being younger she had also forced herself into a pair of pink hot pants and a yellow halter top that

117

probably fit her twenty years ago. Her naked flesh spilled from her provocative attire.

"Would you like to...you know..." she said.

"What?" Joe was baffled. He understood what Mitsy was referring to, but he was having trouble accepting the idea that she believed he could possibly be interested in having sex with her in this doorless room while a rat violently bashed itself against the bathroom door.

There was a moment of awkward silence shared between them. The only noise was the rat attacking the bathroom door. It had obviously worn itself out and it wasn't throwing itself against the door with such vigor. The thuds were less frequent and much less furious.

"What's that noise?" Mitsy asked.

"There is a rat the size of a poodle in the bathroom," exclaimed Joe.

"Oh," said Mitsy. She didn't seem surprised by either the presence of the rat or its abnormal size. "So would you like to have a little...you know...hanky panky."

"Not right now," said Joe.

"What about a drink, then?" She wrestled a flask from her hot pants.

The bathroom was silent. Joe let go of the door and tested it to make sure that it was closed properly and couldn't open.

"I think you've got the wrong room."

"Maybe," said Mitsy as she took a sip from the flask, "but your door was open."

"There is no door," said Joe irritated by Mitsy's lack of observation.

"Oh,." Mitsy turned around and saw that, in fact, the room had

118

no door. "Well, I'll come back to see how you're doing in a little while," she promised Joe as if she were his nurse checking on his "condition."

Joe said nothing he simply watched her slowly wander off.

Joe's Ill-Conceived Plan

Joe pulled out the N0-T4U-2C from his briefcase, sat down on the wooden stool and began reading aloud, "Step 1. Confusion. Confused subversive agents make mistakes. So, confuse them and let them trip over their own two feet." But how, he thought. How can I confuse him? What do I have to do?

Joe began to pace and tried to solve the riddle of the N0-T4U-2C. He brainstormed, but every idea that came to him he had already thought of before and had rejected. He needed something new. Something fresh. Joe sat back down on the stool, closed his eyes and massaged his temples. Like Aladdin rubbing his magic lamp in order to conjure the genie, Joe sat and rubbed. Nothing. He couldn't think of a thing.

He began to think of who he could call for help. Maybe he should call Schmeltz? But calling a supervising agent at 11:00 o'clock at night for help was not something you would expect from an agent of Joe's caliber. What about the Michigan field office? Maybe they could help? But the N0-T4U-2C was a classified document? How could he possibly consult another agent?

He picked up the protocol and began to read it over. "You piece of crap," Joe suddenly howled at it. He threw it on the floor. He jumped up and down on it. He then picked it up from the floor and ripped it in half. He took the ripped pages and crumpled them into balls and threw them around the room, screaming, "You piece of crap."

119

Mitsy was walking by Joe's room when she saw him wrestling with the protocol. "Are you OK?" she asked.

"I'm fine," Joe snapped.

Mitsy stood in the doorway watching Joe. "Maybe you could use that drink now?"

Joe turned on her with wild eyes, "Give me that flask."

Again Mitsy wrestled it from her pants. She handed it to Joe. Joe was about to take a drink, stopped himself and thoroughly cleaned the mouth of the flask with his shirt sleeve and then took a long slow drink.

"Ahhhh," he said as he passed the flask back to Mitsy.

"So, are you ready for a little hoochie coochie action?" asked Mitsy batting her eyelashes seductively.

"Let me ask you a question," Joe felt that there was nothing to lose, "how would you confuse someone? I mean, if you wanted to confuse someone...because let's say...you wanted to take something from them and...confusing them would make it easier...how would you confuse them?"

"I don't know," said Mitsy. She found the question boring, and she lit a cigarette.

"Look who I'm asking for advice," Joe said turning away from Mitsy. He slumped down on the stool at the foot of the bed. He looked like a boxer who had just lost a fight.

"Well, you could put them in a room with no door and ask them to close the door." said Mitsy coolly, taking a drag from her cigarette.

Bingo. Joe's eyes popped open. Revelation. "That's it," he was ecstatic, "It's so simple. You give somebody two contradictory sets of instructions to follow...why didn't I think of that?" He walked

120

excitedly back to Mitsy, grabbed her by the arm and pulled her into the room. "Finally," she said.

"I've got a great idea." Joe took out a pen and a pad of paper from his briefcase and began to write furiously. Mitsy seated herself on the bed and instructed Joe, "You can kiss me anywhere except the lips. The lips are off limits."

Joe wasn't listening to Mitsy He was absorbed in what he was writing. He finished and sat down next to her. "This is what we'll do," he said as he handed her the page he had written. Mitsy started to read it over and said, "Oh, you're one of those weirdos that likes role playing?"

"No. I need your help. I've written a script. All you need to do is call here tomorrow at noon and read your lines."

"Why?"

"Because I need your help," Joe insisted with a smile. "Can we go over the script?"

Mitsy said with great uncertainty, "OK."

"OK, The phone rings and I answer it. Hello. Your line now..."

Mitsy read stiffly, "ObiWan?"

"Yes?"

"This is Darth Vader...Is this some sort of practical joke or something?" she asked without a smile.

"Just stick to the script. Let's keep going," said Joe nearly giggling with excitement.

Mitsy sighed and then continued, "This is Darth Vader. I'm watching you ObiWan. Creamed corn or applesauce?"

"You need to pay attention. It isn't creamed corn *OR* applesauce. It's creamed corn *AND* applesauce."

"Oh, my god…" protested Mitsy.

"And you don't ask. You aren't a waiter taking his order. Tell him creamed corn and applesauce. Let's go through it again."

"Do I have to be Darth Vader? I never liked *Star Wars*."

"It's important that you are Darth Vader because this guy calls himself ObiWan."

"Alright," said Mitsy as she sidled up closer to Joe and whispered, "Remember anywhere but the lips." She put her arm around his shoulder and her tongue in his ear.

Rex Wars

Joe had a restless night. He didn't sleep in the hotel for obvious reasons. Instead, he tried to sleep in the rental car. But for most of the night he couldn't get comfortable. Once he was able to finally drift off to sleep it was early morning and every now and then a delivery van, or some other large vehicle, would pass by, waking him up. So, Joe wrestled with sleep for a couple of hours before his travel alarm started buzzing at 9:00 am. He looked at himself in the rear view mirror. His eyes were red, his face unshaved, his hair a mess.

Since he had some time to kill he decided to have breakfast at the Greasy Burger Diner. After reading the morning paper, drinking a couple cups of coffee, eating scrambled eggs and bacon, Joe felt ready for ObiWan.

He returned to his car and waited. Joe watched the entrance to the hotel with the photo of Fred Bower on his lap. He couldn't believe that the photo he was given was so poor. He made a mental note that he would have to file an official complaint to Schmeltz when he returned regarding the photo. But Joe had confidence that he wouldn't need the photo anyway. He would know his man when he arrived.

All morning long, no one either entered or exited the hotel. At 11:55 am, though, a midget strolled up to the entrance of the Rex Hotel, stopped, looked around and then quickly pushed open the door and slipped inside. "ObiWan," thought Joe.

Joe waited for a couple minutes before following after the midget. Inside the hotel, the bartender was stretched out, as much as possible for a hunchback to stretch out, on the countertop of the bar. Joe asked quietly, "Did someone just come in here for room number 15?"

The bartender nodded and hiccuped, "No funny business. You and the midget have the room for an hour. Not a minute more."

Joe climbed the stairs to the room. He walked briskly down the hall and stopped outside of the doorless room number 15. He knocked on the wall and called out with a whisper, "ObiWan?"

"In here," whispered the little man from inside the room. Joe squinted and saw that ObiWan was lying on the bed. Joe went inside, held up his briefcase and sang seductively, "I have something you want."

ObiWan sat up and mumbled, "I think this was a bad idea. I've got a bad feeling about this. I think I was followed here..."

"You're being paranoid. No one followed us here." Joe then changed the subject, "Do you know that this DVD shows a couple of Senators talking about Project Dead Duck?" Joe opened his briefcase and pulled out the DVD.

"So what?" sputtered the small man.

Shocked, Joe replied, "So what? They know you know."

"Who knows?" asked ObiWan completely confused.

"The Senators on this tape."

"What do they know?"

"They know about Project Dead Duck," Joe said impatiently.

"Why do they care about project dead duck?" complained a frustrated ObiWan.

"What are you talking about?" said Joe unable to understand why the conversation was going so badly.

Before Joe could say anything else, the phone rang. Joe felt relieved. Maybe this will do the trick, he thought grinning to himself.

"You better answer the phone," said Joe to ObiWan.

"Me? Why me?" ObiWan responded.

Joe hadn't given this much thought in the planning phase of this operation. He had simply assumed that ObiWan would answer the phone.

"You're closer to the phone..." Joe said feebly.

"So what? You're taller," said ObiWan.

The little man had a point. Even standing on the bed he couldn't reach the phone. So, Joe put down his briefcase, walked over to the phone and answered it.

"ObiWan?" droned Mitsy.

Joe handed ObiWan the phone and said, "It's for you."

ObiWan cautiously took the phone. He shook with fear as he held it to his ear.

"ObiWan?" said Mitsy again.

"How did you know my name?" ObiWan stammered.

"The guy you're with told me," admitted Mitsy.

"Yoda?" said ObiWan surprised and shocked.

"I don't know his name. Is he a tallish guy with grayish hair, wearing a darkish suit?"

ObiWan turned towards Joe, looked at him carefully and said into the receiver, "Yeah, that's him."

124

"Yeah, he told me. Actually, can I talk to him for a second? " asked Mitsy.

"Sure," said ObiWan suspiciously eying Joe. "It's for you," he said handing the phone back to Joe.

"Me?" choked Joe.

"You seem surprised," commented ObiWan sarcastically.

Joe took the phone and held it to his ear. Mitsy began, "I lost the script you gave me so I thought I'd call to see what you want me to do. I can ad-lib it if you want me to."

"I think you've got the wrong number," said Joe and he hung up the phone. "The wrong number," he reassured ObiWan.

"Really? She knew exactly what you looked like. She also knew my name. And she said you told her my name," said ObiWan as he folded his arms across his chest.

"Maybe you're right," said Joe with a whisper, feigning paranoia, "Maybe we are being watched,"

ObiWan didn't fall for it though. "Forget about it," he said.

The miniature agent was getting ready to storm off when Joe jumped in front of the doorway. ObiWan tried to get around Joe. He moved right, but Joe moved right. He moved left, Joe moved left. Frustrated, he yelled, "Would you get out of my way you...you... loony bastard."

Now it's getting personal, thought Joe. So, he retaliated. With the seriousness of a Hollywood action hero delivering the zinger just before slaughtering a bad guy, Joe said, "So, how about a little trip back to Munchkin Land?"

With that he grabbed ObiWan by the shoulders. Joe's plan was to pick up the tiny man and throw him against the wall. But ObiWan wasn't very cooperative and he was heavier than Joe anticipated. He struggled and Joe had trouble getting a good grip. ObiWan kicked, bit and spat at Joe. As the two wrestled, ObiWan inadvertently delivered a blow to Joe's privates. Joe crumpled to the floor.

ObiWan spat on the gasping Joe and said, "Good riddance." With that, he left the room running.

Joe slowly pulled himself up, he took a couple of deep breaths and ran after the diminutive subversive agent.

Joe ran out of the room, jumped down the surreal staircase, fell through the curtain, quickly picked himself up and ran past the bar where the bartender was reclining. He pushed open the duct taped glass door and stood on the sidewalk outside the hotel surveying Main Street for some sign of ObiWan. Suddenly, he spotted the little man across the street. ObiWan was hiding behind a tree. He saw Joe and knew that Joe had seen him, so he started running. Keeping his eyes on ObiWan, Joe started to dash across the street. Cars screeched to a halt, horns blared and drivers cursed at him as he tried to cross the road. But one blue Dodge Eris, racing down Main Street like a bowling ball hurtling towards a one pin spare, came from out of nowhere. Joe never saw the car coming. He bounced off the windshield and was sent flying. He somersaulted through the air and landed head first on the pavement and laid there in a heap, unconscious.

An Unplanned Collision?

Edgar and Shem had been searching for the stolen ransom money since the end of their botched kidnapping of Angie Quagmire. The hit men that had shown up at the drop-off unexpectedly, and who stole the ransom money, had mentioned a name. This name was ablaze in Edgar's mind: *Ron Frigs*.

126

The two decrepit and aged criminals had spent weeks trying to find Ron Frigs, and when they eventually found him, Ron Frigs proved to be less then cooperative. At first he claimed that he "knew nothing about any money." As Edgar's questioning of Frigs continued, Frigs seemed to think it was some sort of joke. "Is this some sort of shakedown? Did that idiot Pung set you up to this?" he asked with an irritated impersonation of a smile. Edgar decided, then and there, that Frigs needed to be taught a lesson regarding cooperation. With the help of Shem, Frigs was knocked out and loaded into the trunk of the car.

Edgar and Shem were speeding towards the shack at the end of the dirt road in order to further discuss the matter of the missing money with Ron Frigs, albeit in a more secluded location (so secluded, in fact, that screams and shouting would go unheard), when they ran over Joe. Edgar slammed on the brakes and the car skidded to a stop. Thinking that he had run over a dog, Edgar rolled down the window and poked his head out, "Get that bum out of the road." He couldn't understand why someone was lying in the street. Maybe he fainted because the dog was his, Edgar thought.

A small crowd of people began to attend to Joe, clogging the road, barring Edgar's way. A fat, bird faced woman yelled at Edgar, "You just ran over that man."

"Damn it," muttered Edgar as he stepped out of the car and walked to where Joe laid in the street. Edgar had to make sure that this situation was handled gracefully. He didn't want to attract attention and he certainly didn't want anyone to call the police, especially since he had Ron Frigs in the trunk of the car.

"He'll be fine," said Edgar looking at Joe.

"But he's bleeding," responded the woman. In fact, Joe was bleeding. A puddle of blood was forming around his head.

"It's just a scratch," said Edgar turning away.

"I'll call for help," said the woman pulling out a cell phone.

Edgar stopped in his tracks. "No," he spat. He thought for a moment and then turned to the woman and said, "I'll take the bastard to the hospital."

Edgar drove the car to where Joe laid in the street, nearly hitting the old lady in the process.

"Watch where you're going," she shrieked and slapped the car. Edgar, of course, wanted to run over the old, bird faced lady, but he realized that the distance he had to travel, approximately 10 feet, was not long enough for him to get the car moving with the required speed to either seriously harm or kill the old woman.

Edgar stepped out of the car and picked out a bystander from the crowd, a middle aged man pushing a baby stroller. "You," said Edgar pointing his bony finger in the direction of the man. "Put him in the car."

The old woman immediately interjected, "You can't move him."

"Why not?" howled Edgar turning red with frustration.

"He might have a neck injury," snapped the old woman.

"He's fine," said Edgar ferociously. "Now put him in the car."

Edgar knew that he needed to speed things up. He was wasting too much time. He needed to leave before the cops arrived.

"Hurry up," Edgar ordered the man trying to load Joe into the car. The man struggled and strained with Joe's inanimate body, trying hard to keep his clothes clean from blood in the process.

The old woman, who had been preoccupied with the accident until now, had turned her attention to the Blue Dodge Eris and its other occupant: Shem. "What's his story?" she asked pointing at Shem with

128

a disgusted look on her face.

"Shut up you old hag," Edgar came to Shem's defense.

The old woman frowned and then replied flippantly, "You're no spring chicken yourself."

"OK," announced the man that had been struggling to put Joe in the car. He was breathing a bit heavy from his labor and his hands were red with blood. He winced as he looked down at his hands. "He's in the car."

Edgar peered into the backseat and saw Joe lying face down. Edgar climbed into the car, and without another word he punched the gas and disappeared down the road.

The Hyperbole of a Triangle...

As Edgar and Shem sped recklessly down the road, Shem kept peering over his shoulder at Joe who laid on the backseat of the car. Shem seemed uncomfortable about the amount of blood that oozed from Joe's head.

Edgar, sensing Shem's discomfort, said softly, "Don't worry. We'll take care of him after we take care of Frigs."

Edgar drove out to the outskirts of town and pulled off the main road, onto a small dirt lane. He drove quickly down the dirt road. The car jostled up and down with each hole or bump.

The road ended at an old wooden shack. Edgar stopped the car. He and Shem got out and popped the trunk. Ron Frigs was curled up in the fetal position, completely unconscious.

Shem closed his eyes, placed his hands over Ron Frigs and started to chant. Slowly, Ron Frigs regained consciousness. He whispered, barely audible, the somewhat mathematical rambling, "The hyperbole of a triangle is equal to distance with a dash of thyme."

129

The Lost Barfly

As Edgar tried to extract information regarding his missing money from the groggy and incoherent Ron Frigs, Joe slowly began to wake up. As his eyes opened, he, oddly enough, believed that he was the palindromically named accountant Hank Nah from the film *The Lost Barfly*.

Now, *The Lost Barfly*, was a film about an infrequently sober accountant, who believed he was an FBI Agent caught in an infinite loop, always repeating the same sets of experiences over and over again. It was advertised with the truly miserable tag line, *Do until true does not equal true*. Very few understood it.

Joe's (or Hank Nah's for that matter) head erupted with a violent pain. It was as if a wrecking ball was swinging wildly inside his skull and with each destructive stroke he cringed and bit his lip. Joe, thought, I must've got real drunk last night. His mind was a mess of half demolished thoughts and unthinkable debris.

He laid on the seat and tried to will the pain away, but his meditations were interrupted by angry voices coming from somewhere. He looked around and realized that he was in the backseat of a car. He had no idea where he was, and he had no recollection of how he had got there. But there he laid in the backseat of a strange car, in a strange place. And someone had bled all over him.

Joe crept out of the car on his hands and knees, slowly, carefully, trying to keep the brutal wrecking ball silent. As he pushed open the door and emerged from the car he saw that there were three men standing outside, two of which were like ancient relics from a lost era. One of the old men was interrogating what seemed to be a blind man.

"Hey, do any of you guys got a drink?" Joe interrupted,

rubbing his sore head.

Edgar and Shem turned in the direction of Joe. Edgar frowned silently. Ron Frigs asked hopefully, "Who said that? Is there someone else here?"and then Ron screamed, "HHHHHEEEEELLLLLPPPPP."

Ron's screaming sent the wrecking ball back into full swing. Joe braced himself against the car and winced with pain. This was no ordinary hangover. He began to wonder if he had gotten desperate and drank anti-freeze or some other deadly concoction the night before.

"What's going on here?" asked Joe sourly.

"These men have abducted me and now I'm blind," yelled Ron Frigs frantically, nearly in tears.

"It's none of your business," barked Edgar. "Hit the road."

"Listen old man, I need a ride to the nearest bar. And Fast"

"Don't leave me with these lunatics," begged Ron Frigs.

Edgar studied Joe quietly for a moment, looking him up and down and then said, "I'll get you to a bar on one condition: you beat out of this turd where my money is."

Joe squinted in the direction of Ron Frigs and agreed painfully, "OK."

The Interrogation

Joe Lillywhite had been trained in the art of Violent Information Extraction, or VIEX for short. In his right mind, he could have easily rigged up some method of VIEX using a car battery, shoelaces and a menthol cigarette. But because he was incapable of coherent Joe-Lillywhite-thinking (he was only capable of producing muddled Hank-Nah-thoughts), Joe employed a strangely primitive and rather crude method for extracting information from Ron Frigs. He found a thin stick on the ground in front of him. He picked it up and

131

began.

"You stole money from these old people?"

Whack. He hit Ron Frigs like he was a pinata.

"Ouch," yelled Ron Frigs, blindly trying to back away from Joe. He stumbled and fell to the ground. "No. I have no idea what they're talking about."

"How much?"

Whack.

"I told you I didn't steal any money..."

Whack.

"He's lying." Edgar, enjoying the *Punch and Judy* quality of the interrogation, yelled out, "Hit him again"

Whack.

"Ouch. HHHHHEEEEELLLLLPPPPP !!!!! Someone save me."

Whack Whack Whack Whack Whack.

Ron was crying. He looked up and blindly said the first lie that came to him, "OK, I know where the money is. George Pung has it. He works at FUD Alloys, on Fifth Street. Just stop hitting me."

Joe dropped the stick to the ground. His head was pounding and throbbing with pain. The wrecking ball was swinging violently, and his mouth was dry. He walked to the car, opened the passenger door, collapsed into the seat and lost consciousness.

Edgar and Shem climbed into the car. As the blue Dodge Eris sped away, Ron begged blindly, "Please, just leave me alone."

Back at the Rex Hotel

Edgar was thrilled with the turn of events. He felt that he was only a short, five minute drive away from the money. Once the

132

$500,000 was his, the first thing Edgar planned was to buy the necessary materials to build a bomb strong enough to blow the pristine and placid Quagmire house into orbit (with Dr. Quagmire inside of course). Maybe even a few of the neighboring houses would be destroyed as well? How wonderful, thought Edgar.

But because of the proximity of the money, Edgar also began to feel a little nervous. He didn't want anything to get in his way. So, he reasoned that it would be too risky to take Joe to the hospital. Police tended to lurk around hospital hallways. He decided that the best place for Joe was the Rex Hotel. So, Edgar and Shem deposited Joe at the Rex before continuing their quest for missing money.

The bartender was unhappy that Joe had returned. But he was especially irritated that Joe was both unconscious and covered in blood.

Mitsy, seeing Joe's bloody body, said happily, "I knew he would come back." She then begged the old, hunchbacked bartender to allow Joe to stay. The bartender agreed reluctantly and threatened, "If he isn't awake tomorrow morning, I'll have him pitched out with the trash."

Mitsy and a drunk that frequented the bar, Chuck, carried Joe up to room #15. They plopped him down on the bed and covered him with a stained sheet and a blanket full of cigarette burns. Mitsy went to find some towels or rags to clean the blood off of Joe, but she was only able to find an old filthy red bucket with a dry and dusty mop. Apparently, the mop hadn't been used in decades. She filled the bucket with water and brought it to Joe's room.

She splashed water on his face with the mop and did her best to remove some of the blood from his hair. Chuck oversaw the operation drunkenly. "He looks a lot better now," he said as Mitsy put the mop down.

Joe's Visitor

A couple of days after Joe had been brought to the Rex Hotel, a strange and darkly dressed man arrived looking for him. When the man entered the bar, the room full of drunks let out a collective gasp. It was clear to one and all that the man in their presence represented The Authority.

The bartender, who hated everything associated with law and order, spat, "We don't serve your kind here." He pointed to a wooden sign hanging above the bar, "No Feds Allowed."

The strange man ignored the bartender and marched sullenly to the bar. He pulled a photograph from his coat pocket and handed it to the bartender.

"Have you seen this man?" he said with a voice shrouded in mystery.

The bartender looked at the photo. It was a photo of Joe sitting at a desk, working. The bartender would have liked nothing more than to get rid of Joe, but his disdain for authority figures easily persuaded him to keep silent. "No. Never." He handed the photo back to the dark and foreboding stranger.

The strange man then turned in the direction of a group of drunks sitting at the bar. "How about you? Do any of you recognize *this man*." He held the photo up, but no one responded. "His name is Joseph K. Lillywhite," he added. No one responded. "Anyone?" he asked earnestly.

He repeated, "Joseph K," paused for dramatic effect, looked around the bar and resumed "Lillywhite."

"Is he related to Danny Kaye?" asked Chuck taking a sip from his beer.

"Is Danny K. a character from a Franz Kafka novel?"asked the strange man knowing full well that Danny Kaye had never made an appearance in any Franz Kafka novel.

"A Frank Kakfa *what*?" asked Chuck squinting drunkenly.

The stranger could no longer tolerate the conversation with Chuck. He turned his attention to the bartender, "Well, if you do see this man, then you can contact me at the number on this card." He handed the bartender a business card, and turned to leave.

"Who the hell are you?" asked Chuck.

The strange man paused at the door for a moment, his back to the bar, and said, "I have come on behalf of someone very powerful in order to make sure that certain things go by unseen." He disappeared as suddenly as he had appeared.

Joe Returns

After five days of weaving in and out of consciousness, Joe woke up with a burp. As he sat up, Mitsy put out her cigarette and exclaimed, "You're awake. It's a miracle."

Without understanding where he was or why a woman with a handlebar mustache would be so excited that he would wake up, Joe said, "I'm parched sister. How about a drink?"

Mitsy took Joe by the arm and helped him down the hallway. She tenderly led him down the stairs, pulled back the red velvet curtain and there, through the doorway, Joe saw heaven. The room was a cloud of smoke, smelled like a damp carpet and a couple of drunks were already sitting at the bar preparing for the destruction the new day promised. He clapped his hands and rubbed them together with delight as he entered the lounge of the Rex Hotel.

"Good morning boys and girls," he said as Mitsy helped him onto a bar stool. "What's for breakfast?" he asked the bartender playfully.

The old bartender smirked and said, "Some one came looking for you while you were snoozing up there in one of my rooms." He was angry and he spat as he talked.

"Looks like someone got up on the wrong side of the bed this morning," Joe said to Mitsy with a wink.

The bartender pushed a business card to Joe. Joe picked it up and read a name, "Fred Deller. Hmmm," he pulled at his chin. "What'd he look like?"

"He was tallish with glasses. Brown hair," grunted the bartender.

"He was blond," corrected a drunk named Cheryl.

"And I wouldn't call him tall, more like average height," said Chuck.

"So, he was average height to tall with either brown or blond hair?" Joe inquired.

"He definitely had glasses," said Cheryl.

"Ah yes, with glasses." Joe got up from his seat. He swaggered a bit and smiled slyly. "He's my nemesis. A Russian agent. A commie. He took his poodle to the Smithsonian and he let it hump Ben Franklin's wooden leg in front of a school of third graders on a field trip. He's a real bastard."

"I didn't know you could bring poodles into the Smithsonian," Chuck whispered to Cheryl.

"His presence means only one thing – the cat and mouse game continues. Life goes on. Let's have a drink!" Joe grabbed a bottle of whiskey from the bar and started to guzzle it down. The bartender

136

wrestled it free from Joe, spilling whiskey all over the countertop and down the front of Joe's shirt. Joe jumped up on the bar and in classic Hank Nah style prepared to sing the chorus from *Don't Cry for Me Argentina,* but the words to the song could not be conjured from Joe's faulty memory. Instead, he substituted what he believed were his own words, but it was actually a variation of the third law of Tc

> Confuse people to such an extent
> They cannot tell truth from fiction.
> If you can do this
> Then you are heading in the right direction.

As Joe sang and danced on the countertop of the bar, no one said a word. Everyone held their glasses in their hands, wondering who the lunatic was that was waltzing and singing.

The bartender slapped at Joe's legs trying to force him off the bar. But Joe's celebratory dance could not be interrupted. He called out, "Come on! Everyone sing!"

Chuck raised an eyebrow and pondered, "Maybe I should switch to Vodka."

OOPS, Inc.

T his was a big mistake, thought Jamie Dropping as Evan and Ivan scurried around the office opening windows, cleaning up the coffee that had been thrown on the fire, and squawking and swearing in a desperate state of frustrated anger. The Receptionist, who had been alerted of the fire by a string of brutal obscenities from Evan, stood in the doorway, fanning away the smell of the burning paper with her hand. "What happened in here?" she asked coughing.

Well, what had happened in Evan and Ivan's office was the overly melodramatic resignation of a disgruntled employee named Roy Deedle. Deedle had worked as a technical writer for the past two months, during which time he had come to the conclusion that those two months were the worst of his 36 year life, even worst than the time he had been inadvertently buried alive when he was 5 years old.

After Deedle had barged into the office, he proclaimed,

"Working here has been as painful as having the shingles." He then set a document on fire in effigy. The document was supposed to represent Evan and Ivan or maybe it represented the Job. In any case, as the flames began to quickly consume the pages, Roy dropped the flaming document on Evan's desk and said slowly, loudly and emphatically, so no one would miss his meaning, "GO TO HELL."

During this dramatic conflagration of human unhappiness, Jamie sat in a chair near Evan's desk, his mouth hanging open, clutching his briefcase to his chest, telling himself, this was a big mistake.

Ms. Lucy Doff 's Yuletide Debauchery

The day of Roy Deedle's fiery resignation was also Jamie's first day of work for his new employer whose ill-advised name was announced proudly on a sign outside the office

Object Oriented Payment Solutions, Inc.

Just prior to the Roy Deedle drama, Jamie had learned from the Receptionist that the woman who had hired him, Ms. Lucy Doff, had been fired a couple of weeks ago. The Receptionist, a rotund woman sipping a Diet Coke and eating potato chips, was well made-up with enormous fire engine red lips. She seemed ready to betray the most intimate details about Ms. Doff. She began to tell Jamie about Ms. Doff's disastrous accident at the company's Christmas party. "Well, let's just say she and one of Santa's little helpers drank a little too..." Jamie, like a chameleon reacting to its environment, changed expressions from nervous amicability to nervous confusion. He blurted out, "So, who should I talk to if she's been fired?" The Receptionist, clearly insulted that Jamie wasn't interested in Ms. Doff's drunken Yuletide debauchery, said testily, "Well, I guess you'll just need to talk to Evan and Ivan. Won't you?"

With that, she picked up the phone and dialed the internal number for Evan and Ivan's office. "I have a Mr. Dropping here." She listened, nodding in agreement to something she was being told. "OK, OK. But today is Mr. Dropping's *first* day. Ms. Doff hired him." She sang this last part, *Ms. Doff hired him,* with stinging irony. This seemed to be all that needed to be said. With the mention of Ms. Doff, the conversation ended. She hung up the phone and said with a vague smile, "They'll see you immediately."

Just past the Receptionist's desk was the office of the Managing Director, Mr. Bert Trigger. His name was printed in big black block letters across the frosted glass of his office door. Adjacent to his office, was the office occupied by Evan and Ivan. Jamie stopped at their door and knocked with an urgent unsteadiness. After a brief moment of nervous waiting, which Jamie experienced as an uncomfortable eternity, he opened the door and popped his head inside the office. Jamie was prepared to say, "May I come in," but the words dissolved in his mouth. He was stunned silent by what he saw.

The Proxy Pattern

Evan Proxy and Ivan Pattern both looked as if they had just graduated from high school. Jamie saw these "men," with their fresh faces full of youthful blemishes, and thought, they're just children. After the initial shock that Jamie suffered, he slowly realized that both Evan and Ivan resembled each other greatly. They both wore matching dark business suits, shared the same flat-top hairstyle and, as Jamie was soon to realize, also shared the same voice.

Now, Evan and Ivan, both in their early thirties, considered their youthful appearances a curse. Fellow workers, colleagues and other managers tended not to take them seriously. So, in order to make sure that the employees of OOPS understood they meant business, they were typically cruel and ruthless bastards. Once upon a time, they had banished an entire department to the storage area as a punishment for disobeying their order of no eating fish in the company kitchen. A tuna fish sandwich was the official cause of the department's exile.

When Evan and Ivan were hired, they were considered maverick geniuses that could streamline the most untamed operations, untangle inefficient processes and, well, help make the bottom line a little more healthy. Unfortunately, they had not been able to make such a dramatic impact on the culture of OOPS. No one was sure how much longer Evan and Ivan would oversee day to day operations, but most people agreed that "Evan and Ivan put the oops in OOPS" and that "Evan and Ivan put the Inc in Incompetence." For the five years they had been working at OOPS, every day was the same tragedy - budget overruns, missed deadlines, screaming clients, bugs, general mismanaged chaos, aspirin, headaches, panic and fear.

"Mr. Dropping," said Evan from behind his desk, "I am Evan Proxy and this is Ivan Pattern. Please take a seat." Jamie entered the office, closed the door and sat down in a chair near Evan's desk.

"It seems that we have a slight problem here," said Ivan immediately. Their voices were clones of one another. Jamie looked from Evan to Ivan and then back to Evan in disbelief. If you were to close your eyes and simply listen to the two men speak, it would be impossible to tell which of them was actually the source of the words you were hearing.

"What sort of problem?" said Jamie defensively.

"Well, Ms. Doff, the woman that hired you has been..." Evan

142

started to explain.

"I was informed by the receptionist that Ms. Doff was fired. She also explained to me that Ms. Doff took a drunken fancy to Christmas elf. But, frankly gentlemen, I don't see what this has to do with me." Jamie smiled uneasily. He was not about to let these two high schoolers tell him what to do.

"Well, Mr. Dropping," said Evan slightly irritated by Jamie's abruptness, "Ms. Doff was fired for embezzling money. After she was fired, the Managing Director met with us and we rethought the project that she was supposed to be leading. I believe it was called DEJECTUS? Well, anyway, the Managing Director concluded that the project would be postponed indefinitely."

Jamie could feel his face burning red with embarrassment. He felt as though he was the butt of a malicious practical joke. He began to fidget in his chair, crossing and uncrossing his legs, picking pieces of lint off his pants. "I was hired to work on DEJECTUS," he eventually admitted quietly.

"So you understand our problem," snapped Ivan. "You have been hired by a woman that has been fired, to work on a project that does not exist."

Ivan's statement made Jamie fully appreciate his existential uncertainty. But he refused to accept Evan and Ivan's belief that *he* somehow inherited their problems. Clearly, the problem was theirs. So, he began to prepare a defense and was about to rebut Ivan's statement when Roy Deedle stormed in, and within seconds the office was engulfed with smoke.

As Jamie sat in the cloud of smoke, cradling his briefcase in his arms, wondering what in the world was going on, his wife's ghost suddenly appeared. It wasn't the first time he had seen her ghost, but it was the first time she had appeared outside of his apartment. "I told you not to work for a company called OOPS," she scolded him. Just as quickly as she had materialized, she vanished.

Jamie began to feel as though he were a fictional character in some sort of unbelievable narrative. He sat motionlessly staring at Evan and Ivan as they raced about. He had a faraway look in his eyes that suggested that no stimuli could possibly reach him. He was staring blanks.

Neither Evan nor Ivan appreciated that Jamie just sat there doing nothing. At one point, Evan yelled at him, "Don't just sit there, do something." With those words, Jamie was yanked from his vacant thoughts and he stood up immediately. But he didn't know what to do, so he simply stood there, cradling his briefcase in his arms. Then Evan exploded, and words vulgar and putrid flew from of his mouth like a flock of birds bursting into flight.

The Receptionist appeared in the doorway. "What happened here?" she asked fanning the smoke from her face and coughing.

"Roy Deedle happened here," snarled Ivan waving his arms frantically in order to disperse the smoke.

The receptionist slipped away with a disapproving shake of her head, and within a couple of minutes returned with a blue cloaked cleaning woman. The cleaning woman started to furiously mop up the spilled coffee from the floor, then she cleaned the coffee from Evan's desk.

As the smoke began to clear and the chaos began to settle, Evan told Jamie, "Mr. Dropping, we will have to put this matter to the Managing Director. He should be in the office later today. He will decide your fate." Both Evan and Ivan wore the same smug look on their faces that indicated to Jamie that the door to this conversation

144

was closed. Jamie reasoned that they just wanted to clean up their embarrassment as quickly and quietly as possible.

"Take him down to the technical documentation department," said Evan to the Receptionist. She sighed and rolled her eyes.

"But I'm a software engineer not a technical writer," protested Jamie vainly.

"Stop that! You're only making it worse," Ivan blared at the cleaning woman who was spraying a lemon scented air freshener around the room. The room smelled of sweet, smoky lemons which obviously displeased Ivan.

"Go on, take him," said Evan irritated that neither Jamie or the Receptionist had budged.

Jamie said nothing else. He no longer had the desire to squabble with Evan and Ivan. These men, like all managers are completely out of touch with reality, Jamie thought. He hoped to have better luck with the Managing Director. Plus, he reasoned, if the Managing Director would decide his "fate" later that day, then what did it matter if he spent the day as a technical writer?

As Jamie turned to leave, Evan called him, "Oh, one more thing Mr. Dropping. Tell Mr. Closing that Roy Deedle has been fired."

What a putz, thought Jamie.

Technical Documentation

Jamie was escorted to the Technical Documentation Department by the Receptionist. She clearly did not want to take Jamie, and after Jamie had left Evan and Ivan's office she stayed behind to remind Evan and Ivan that it wasn't her job to escort the likes of Jamie Dropping anywhere, especially the Technical Documentation Department. She had infinitely more important things to do. Evan and

Ivan pressed her into service, though, because they wanted to make sure Jamie found the Technical Documentation Department and remained there. "The important thing is that he *remain* there," Evan explained. Neither he nor Ivan wanted Jamie to resurface again for the rest of the day. The Receptionist told them that she would escort Mr. Dropping to the basement under protest. They paid her no mind. They simply desired Jamie's immediate absence.

Jamie lagged behind the receptionist as she led him down a narrow spiral staircase to the basement. They descended in what could only be described as hostile amicability. Jamie found the silence a bit uncomfortable, and so he decided that he would make an attempt to repair their damaged relationship. "So, she and the elf had sex?"

"What are you talking about?" She was obviously irritated that he had broken the silence.

Jamie thought for a moment about clarifying who and what he was talking about, but he didn't have the courage. He felt that if he were to say much more the Receptionist might viciously beat him.

She led and Jamie followed.

At the bottom of the stairs the Receptionist waited for Jamie. As Jamie exited the steps, he found himself in what appeared to be nothing more than a storage room. Bookshelves, crammed with books and binders, were anchored to the walls of the room. Books spilled off the shelves. Beige file cabinets were stationed randomly throughout the room with no apparent attention to efficient use of space. Atop two of the file cabinets stood broken computer monitors which made the file cabinets resemble some sort of primeval corporate totem poles. There were a couple of large cardboard boxes that were open and overflowing with paper. At the far end of the room was a large table and on the table sat three computers.

As Jamie was taking in this strange landscape in front of him, the Receptionist, clearing her throat loudly, announced, "You have a newcomer."

This sudden and unexpected outburst startled Jamie. He gave the Receptionist a quizzical glance and wondered who she thought she was speaking to. But then Jamie saw them. He hadn't been able to see them since they sat behind the computers at the large table in the center of the room, but people inhabited this land of junk and debris. A man and a woman were now peering at him from over the tops of their monitors. He could clearly make out the tops of their heads and their eyes.

The Receptionist, pushed her way past Jamie and started to climb the stairway. She stopped at the second step and said with a glib smile, "Welcome to the heart of darkness."

The Man They Called Chewbacca

One of the natives of the Technical Documentation Department, that had been sitting behind a computer, ventured out to meet Jamie. His name was Steve, but his colleagues in the Technical Documentation Department called him Chewbacca because he was gruff, smelled awful and usually moaned loudly about everything and anything.

Steve was a shrub shaped man with a peculiar sense of fashion. His white pressed business shirt was two times too large for him and the shoulders floated around the area of his biceps. He had to wear the shirt sleeves rolled-up simply to expose his hands and eliminate the unsightly clumping of sleeve around his wrists. Steve wore black jeans that were too small, and he was unable to keep them buttoned. His stubborn midsection refused to cooperate. Consequently, his zipper was usually open.

Jamie, who was too shocked by the appearance of the office to move a centimeter from the bottom of the stairs, stood silently watching Steve approach. Steve stopped a couple feet from Jamie, settled into a casually confrontational posture by folding his arms against his chest and leaning back on his heels. He said with a loud and booming voice, "No one told us a new person would start today." Jamie felt awkward as the man examined him with an unfriendly, surgically precise glance.

Jamie explained, "There seems to be a little confusion..." Jamie was prepared to fire off a diatribe against Evan and Ivan implicating them in the most heinous acts of managerial incompetence, when he suddenly realized that this man standing before him was, in fact, bleeding. A trickle of blood ran down his forehead. Jamie shuddered involuntarily at the sight of the blood.

"You're bleeding," he cringed.

Steve pulled a wad of tissue from his pockets and dabbed his forehead. After each dab he examined the tissue. As he cleaned the blood from his forehead he explained, "My doctor removed a lump from my head this morning." He bowed to show Jamie the wound. The top of Steve's head was shaved and a piece of gauze was taped to his scalp. Jamie peered at Steve's head unwillingly and saw some blood trickle out from the gauze. "He wanted to run a biopsy on it."

Jamie shuddered again and silently wondered if he could somehow get his old job back.

Santa's Elf, the Easter Bunny

The second native from behind the computer now joined Jamie and the bleeding Steve. She was small, brunette, bright and buoyant. Her face was adorned with a smile that was a relief to Jamie. She was the first person that he had met this morning that didn't seem miserable. She smiled and offered her hand, "Hello, I'm Jane." Jamie shook her hand. "Jamie Dropping."

"I see you've met Steve already."

Steve refused to shake hands with Jamie. He stood with his arms folded against his chest, rocking on his heels. "So, what happened to Roy?" he growled.

"Roy's been fired." Without thinking about it, Jamie said these words with great sensitivity, as if he was a close friend of Roy's.

"And you're Roy's replacement?" asked Steve pointedly. "Pretty convenient for you isn't it? Someone gets fired and you get hired." He glared accusingly at Jamie.

"No. I'm a software engineer. I was hired by Ms. Doff..."

"She was fired a couple of weeks ago," chortled Steve. "Embezzling."

"I know..." began Jamie.

"Her boyfriend was a midget," Steve added.

Jamie said nothing.

"He worked as one of Santa's elves at Christmas time."

Again, Jamie said nothing.

"He worked as the Easter Bunny in spring."

"You haven't met Edward yet. He's the manager and wordsmith of the department," said Jane changing the subject. Her smile seemed to be a permanent feature of her face. Even as she spoke, it never slipped from place. As she led Jamie towards Edward's office, she suddenly stopped, made sure that Steve wasn't watching and grabbed Jamie's hand. Jamie was surprised by this gesture. He was not a touchy-feely person and he instinctively felt uncomfortable about being fondled in such a personal way. Then he realized that Jane had placed something in his palm. It was a piece of paper. As secretly as possible, he glanced into the palm of his hand and read the message. It said, *"DOES A TOILET FLUSHING IN THE DARK MAKE A SOUND."*

He felt that the message was a bit odd. He didn't know if he should laugh or provide an answer. Seeing that there was no question mark, Jamie reasoned that maybe it wasn't a question after all. The message had the look and feel of a Zen aphorism. Maybe Jane was an aspiring writer of Zen aphorisms, although obviously talentless. Whether the lights are on or off doesn't affect the sound of a toilet flushing. Maybe, it's a trick question of some sort and I should give it more thought, Jamie eventually concluded, and he slipped the paper into his pocket.

Edward Closing

Edward Closing ruled the Technical Documentation Department from a gypsy style construction that was his office. Behind the table where Jane and Steve sat was what appeared to be a partial wall. In reality, it was merely a couple of tall pieces of drywall propped up against file cabinets and cardboard boxes. Behind this drywall facade sat Edward Closing, brooding at his desk.

Edward was 55 years old and had been working for OOPS for the past ten years, the longest of any of the others in the Technical Documentation Department. He was a thin man with a ropy body and a full head of silver hair. He sat at his desk with his shirt sleeves rolled

150

up, his tie slackened, collar unbuttoned, reading a newspaper.

"Edward, we have what appears to be a new person with us," Jane announced.

"Jamie Dropping," said Jamie marching to Edward's desk and holding out his hand.

Edward peered over the top of his bifocals at the approaching Jamie and shook his hand, "Nice to meet you." Looking past Jamie to Jane, he added, "But no one told me anything about a new hire?"

Jamie began to explain his presence, "Well, it's a long and complicated story, so let me simplify it a bit. Roy Deedle just lit some sort of document on fire in Evan and Ivan's office and quit. I was hired to start today and to work with Ms. Doff on a project called DEJECTUS. She, as you know, was fired, and so Evan and Ivan came up with the truly awful decision to send me, a software engineer, to your department to work for the day until the Managing Director can decide where I belong."

"You don't say," said Edward sourly. He examined Jamie carefully, looking him up and down.

"Well, take a seat Jane. You too James. Did you happen to read this morning's news?"

"No." said Jamie enthusiastically. It was obvious, though, that Edward really wanted to speak to Jane and that he regarded Jamie's presence coldly.

"Well it appears that the Quagmire Incident has taken another strange twist." He pushed the paper towards Jane. Jamie leaned towards Jane and they both read the headline ***Dr. Quagmire Recovers Miraculously But Young Angie Vanishes Again.***

"Not again," sighed Jane with a smile.

"Well, that's too bad," said Jamie sitting back in his seat. He, along with all of Ersatz Michigan, had been sucked into the quicksand of the Quagmire Incident at one point or another. But he had grown weary of the story's ins-and-outs, with it's constant airplay and analysis. At this point any news about the Quagmire's was merely anticlimactic. Jamie found the whole thing boring and couldn't understand why people were actually interested any longer.

"The article states that the girl's mother believes that it was the work of aliens. Extra terrestrials. Her daughter was abducted." This last sentence was punctuated by Edward's big, yellow coffee stained smile.

Newspaper Flashback

Historically speaking, the Quagmire Incident began the day that the local Ersatz newspaper, the **Eye of Ersatz,** ran the story *Deranged Man Without Pants Attacks Police in Park*. But no one knew that the pantless man was Dr. Harry Quagmire trying to pay off his daughter's kidnappers.

Nonetheless, a day after the pantless Dr. Quagmire had fought with the police, the **Eye of Ersatz** broke the story *Bizarre Kidnapping Leaves One Injured and Another in a Coma*. Apparently, a young girl named Angie Quagmire had been kidnapped and as she was being returned to her father, for the price of $500,000, a shoot-out ensued. Police found a woman, Mrs. Martha Frigs, shot and unconscious in a wooded area not far from the kidnapping. Angie said that Mrs. Martha Frigs had nothing to do with the kidnapping. She had never even seen her before.

But the real news was that Angie's father fell into a coma as he fought with one of the kidnappers. Angie had a theory regarding his sudden coma, but the **Eye** wasn't interested. It was an outlandish tale.

Strangely enough though, the medical community of Ersatz Michigan concluded that Dr. Quagmire was not comatose. The doctors declared that he was in a "state of suspended animation." When the **Eye** found out that the doctors believed that Dr. Quagmire was in a state of suspended animation, whatever that meant, the reporter rushed back to Angie for an interview. The next day the **Eye** continued the story with the headline *Kidnap Victim's Father in a State of Suspended Animation*. The story reported that one of the kidnappers was in fact some sort of witch doctor. The police made an official statement telling the public that they suspected the use of voodoo and that they were on the lookout for anyone that fit the description of a witchdoctor.

Only a couple of days later, a body was found in the Rex Hotel. A man had been murdered by being drowned in a bathtub full of creamed corn and applesauce. Everyone in Ersatz was shocked about this sudden burst of violence. Kidnapping and murder didn't happen in Ersatz. At least they usually didn't happen in the same week. So, naturally, everyone in Ersatz started getting nervous, especially the police since they had three kidnappers, one of which was a witchdoctor, and a murderer at large.

It wasn't long after these events that the **Eye of Ersatz** reported some animal bones were found in the yard of Little Lamb kindergarten. An elderly lady, Mrs. Kerwitz, who lived near the kindergarten, said that her dog, a poodle named Frank, had been missing for days. "Frank has never gone missing before," she sobbed to the police.

Animal bones? Missing poodles? Dr. Quagmire's voodoo induced coma like state? The authorities could smell the sulphur burning. They created a list of suspects and atop the list was none other than Satan himself. The police were convinced that Ersatz had dived, head first, into the deepest most rotten pit of hell.

A couple of days later, the suspicions of the Ersatz Police Department were confirmed when a couple of high school students that were searching for a quiet and secluded place to "finish their geometry homework," stumbled into "a drunken satanic orgy." The group told police that they were "forced to participate in the fornication" and that "blood was everywhere." Naturally, the police assumed that the blood probably belonged to a recently murdered poodle named Frank.

As things began to heat up in Ersatz and as the city buzzed with fear that was as dangerous as a chain-smoking arson working in a gas station, a priest by the name of Father Patrick asked the simple questions, "Are our children safe? Are they out of harm's way?" As it turned out they weren't. Police rounded up the children from Little Lamb kindergarten in order to interrogate them. They suspected that Mr. Harry Wiener, a teacher at the school, worshiped Satan. To the shock of parents, the police investigation found that all the children at the kindergarten had been molested by Mr. Wiener.

The release of this finding sent Ersatz into a Harry-Wiener-hating, destroy-little-lamb hysteria. Naturally, everyone wanted to see Weiner executed. The Little Lamb kindergarten was burned to the ground.

As the smoke and stench of hell began to thicken, the District Attorney of Ersatz County realized, after reading through the transcripts of the interrogated children, that there was no real case against Mr. Wiener. He explained to the police that some of the questions they asked were slightly problematic, in a legal sense, and forced the children to falsely implicate Harry. "Come on guys," he yelled at the chief of police and the detectives in charge of the case. "This will never stand up in court. Look here, a detective asks a kid,

154

'Are you sure that Harry Wiener molested you more than once?' The kid responds, 'No.' Then the detective asks, and this is brilliant, 'So you aren't sure he molested you more than once? How many times did he molest you then?' The answer 'Three.' Come on guys!"

So it was that the charges were dropped. The police admitted that they believed Mr. Wiener was, unfortunately, innocent of all child molesting charges, although he was still investigated for links to Satan and the illegal practice of Voodoo. But then Frank the poodle returned home, happily wagging his surgically shortened poodle tail. The case was officially closed.

Ms. Kerwitz, who didn't know where Frank was for all those days, told the **Eye of Ersatz** she was just "glad he was alive and that he hadn't been murdered by a bunch of satan worshiping child molesters like Harry Wiener."

DoDis Rides Again

"Extra Terrestrials." Edward seemed ecstatic about this news. He stood up and began to pace about his tiny office with the intensity of a hurricane.

"The mother stated that she heard a strange noise. She went to her husbands bedroom where she found a strange *grey* man standing over top of him chanting. She said there was a *burst* of *bright light* and she was *frozen*. She couldn't *move*. That is all she remembers. She woke up a couple hours later asleep on the floor. The girl hasn't been seen since."

Jamie and Jane watched Edward as he paced. He walked to and fro mumbling to himself. It was clear that he was wrestling with something big. Suddenly, he stopped and seemed to stare through some invisible window that exposed a glorious new universe.

While Edward stood transfixed, Jane leaned towards Jamie and whispered, "Edward has a web site dedicated to the Quagmire Incident. He's obsessed with it."

"What software systems are you documenting currently?" Jamie whispered back.

Jane was taken aback by the question, her smile twitched nervously and she chuckled. "Roy was the only one who actually worked around here."

Edward stopped pacing. He stood motionless as a revelation came crashing into him with the force of a meteor slamming into a planet. "The Department of Disinformation!" he announced pumping the air with a wizened fist.

Ann O'Nymous

Shortly after Edward had launched his site (www.thequagmireincident.com) that presented a "factual day by day analysis of the Quagmire Incident," he was contacted via email by someone that went by the name Ann O'Nymous. It didn't take Edward more than a half hour to realize that Ann O'Nymous was not Irish and that the name was really a playful pseudonym for someone that wanted to remain *anonymous*.

Ann informed Edward that she was a former FBI agent that used to work for the Department of Disinformation. She then began to explain that the information she was providing to Edward was intended for a larger audience. She wanted him to post her information on his website so that the people of Ersatz would "understand what is really going on."

Ann's message to the world was this, "The kidnapping of Angie Quagmire is a fiction. It may have actually happened but it is

156

being constructed and reported in such a way to ensure that other things go by unnoticed. There is a much darker plot at work here. Here are the facts: (1) James Alexander Shade was murdered the night Angie Quagmire was found. (2) James Alexander Shade had written a book titled the *Mass Extinction Event* (I urge all of you to read this book). (3) *The Mass Extinction Event* contains classified information. (4) The FBI sent an agent named Joe Lillywhite to Ersatz Michigan in an attempt to recover classified information that they believed Shade possessed. (5) The FBI Agent, Joe Lillywhite, went missing and has never been found. (6) A second agent, Fred Deller, was sent to find the missing Lillywhite. The day that Deller arrived, the front page news article in the **Eye of Ersatz** was about teenagers stumbling into a drunken satanic orgy (a completely ridiculous and unbelievable story engineered by DoDis in order to thought clog the public in the eventuality that the Lillywhite story would break)..."

There were many, many more facts that Ann reported. In total she listed 258 facts. But she closed with an eerie exhortation, "James Shade's *The Mass Extinction Event* depicts a scenario in which the Government turns war into a reality style TV program. But the program is not for human consumption. The program has been sold to a race of entertainment starved aliens known as QabNoks. These QabNoks are here and working with the Government and Hollywood to create a nuclear war that will be televised throughout the universe. Why? The Universal Governing and Organizing Department (UGOD) thinks that the time for the next mass extinction event on earth is overdue. The residents of this vast universe want to make sure that us *Homo Sapiens* are wiped out before we start exporting our own forms of extinction to other planets." And now the aliens had in fact entered the picture.

The World is Coming to an End and You Want to Work?

"I think it's time to build the ark," said Edward returning to his seat.

"Excuse me?" Jamie had no idea what Edward was talking about.

"The world's coming to an end," Jane whispered smiling.

"If that woman leans over and whispers into your ear one more time, you'll be sorry." Jamie's wife's ghost had appeared again. Her diaphanous face hovered menacingly close to Jamie's. If her nose was real it would have pressed against his. As quickly as she had appeared, she disappeared again.

Jamie had recoiled into his seat. His dead wife's ghost seemed to be getting more and more aggressive. Although she usually never appeared outside of the apartment, she had now made herself visible to Jamie twice at OOPS. He found it very disconcerting.

Now, his dead wife's ghost was not able to do any real harm to anyone or anything. But she could perform annoying pranks, like hide Jamie's car keys. There was one time where she hid Jamie's keys by burying them in the cat's litter box.

"Will somebody please show me to my desk," he blurted out.

"The world is coming to an end and you want to work?" Edward couldn't believe his ears. He already disliked Jamie intensely.

"You can take Roy's seat I guess," Edward said slowly still trying to comprehend why someone would be interested in work when doomsday was probably only hours away. Jamie uncoiled himself and stood up with a sigh of relief. "Maybe you could help Steve with the project he and Roy were working on?" Edward said with a frown.

Jamie was preparing to make a quick exit from Edward's shanty of an office when Jane beamed, "I'll show Jamie to Roy's

158

computer."

"No," barked Edward, "you and I have a few things to discuss."

Jamie was relieved that Jane was detained by Edward. His wife's ghost seemed strangely jealous of Jane, and Jamie was acutely frightened of his dead wife's ghost. Jamie scrambled out of the office.

PUD

Steve was sitting at his computer picking his nose.

"Where's Roy's computer?" Jamie asked.

"Over there," said Steve. Startled by Jamie's sudden appearance, he quickly and discreetly pulled his finger from his nose and pointed in the direction of Roy's computer. Jamie sat down at the computer and found that it was turned on and that Roy had already logged in.

Jamie took a couple of moments to calm himself and then informed Steve, "Edward said I should take a look at the project you and Roy were working on."

Steve looked up at Jamie and asked squinting, "What?"

Jamie repeated himself a little more loudly, "Edward said I should take a look at the project you and Roy were working on."

Jamie noticed for the first time, that Steve would squint at him whenever he spoke. It was as if he was nearsighted and was trying to read the words as they came out of Jamie's mouth. Accompanying Steve's squint was a grimace of sorts that seemed to suggest that he was suffering some kind of pain, as if Jamie's words poked or painfully prodded him.

"Well you can begin by looking at some files on Roy's computer." Steve joined Jamie at Roy's computer and navigated to the location of the files.

"Now these files," explained Steve using the mouse pointer to indicate the files he was referring to, "document the S.E.A. system. This file contains the source code for the program. It might be of interest to you since you're," Steve paused and gave Jamie a cursory glance and resumed, "a programmer."

"I'm a software engineer," corrected Jamie. "What is the S.E.A. System?"

Again, Steve's face was puckered into a painful squint, "It's the data encryption program used in all transaction handling." Steve returned his attention to the files, "This file documents the algorithm used by S.E.A. It's a good starting point," he said as he opened the file. Once the file opened, Steve stared at the computer monitor in disbelief. He closed the file and opened it again. "Hmmm," he said. It struck Steve strange that the file was empty of all content except for one word. And this word stood like a monument in the center of the page.

Pud

"Hmmm," Steve repeated himself. He opened another file, then another file. Eventually, he opened all the files, and they all contained the same single word.

"You must have a virus," concluded Steve.

Jamie knew this was no virus. This was a premeditated act of vandalism.

"This is not good," grunted Steve.

"Don't you have any backups?" asked Jamie hopelessly.

Steve shook his head, "No. But we do have hard copies of these files..."

Steve went to a bookshelf and jerked out a white binder that was firmly wedged between other white binders. Licking his index finger and his thumb, he began to page through the binder. As he turned the pages, it became clear to Jamie that what Steve was looking for was missing. Steve would stop and backtrack. He had a puzzled look on his face. Steve went back to the bookshelf and he stared at the countless white binders. A trickle of blood ran down his forehead.

Poop-Text

Steve searched through numerous white binders. The back of his shirt, around his collar, was wet with sweat, and pools of sweat had collected at his armpits. He stood hunched over the latest binder he had taken from the bookshelf, dabbing his forehead with his wad of tissues.

"Aha," said Steve suddenly. "I've found something." He put the binder in front of Jamie who had been concentrating desperately not to think about anything that his wife's ghost might find offensive. He was afraid that his dead wife would make an unwanted appearance again. His right hand was buried in his pants pocket firmly clutching

162

his car keys.

"This is the source code for the S.E.A. system," said Steve with a sweaty smile.

Jamie said nothing as he returned from the faraway land of his psychic turmoil. "It's written in a language called Cod," Steve explained.

"Cod? I've never heard of it," said Jamie. He looked at the page of code and nearly wept. The first line read,

a(em%12;-fuDx2mch;9yt$(b[em%poo;vary;x]))=fred.

"Are you serious?"

"Oh yeah, that's Cod," said Steve.

Steve flipped past the pages of source code and he stopped at another page of plain text and said, "And this is an example of the encrypted text. Roy called it 'poop-text.'"

As Jamie read the text he understood why Roy had called it *poop-text*. It was a rather long story containing incoherent and freakish characters, and filled with references to the scatological. Poop and toilets abounded.

"Are you sure this is the encrypted text?"

"Yeah," Steve said simply. "S.E.A. Scatological Encryption Algorithm," he added with a shrug as if it were obvious.

"Scatological Encryption Algorithm?" choked Jamie. He couldn't believe what he was being told. "This is not the encrypted text," he insisted. "This is probably what was used *for* encryption. It's some sort of silly joke."

Jamie tried to hand the page back to Steve, but Steve was not in the mood to take it. He was irritated by Jamie's disbelief. He stood motionlessly. Jamie shook the paper impatiently at Steve and said, "Here, take it."

"It *is* the encrypted text," protested Steve. "Hold the paper to the light."

"Hold it to the light?" The idea was preposterous.

"Hold it to the light," moaned Steve loudly.

Jamie sighed and held the paper to the light. Steve looked at the paper eagerly. "Do you see it?" Jamie was irritated beyond words.

"See what?" he asked dully.

"The original text."

Jamie looked at the paper and was astounded. He could clearly see words contained in the words of the poop-text. Floating about in the shadows of the poop-text was a subtext, the original text.

Jamie took a moment to think and said, "Wait a second. The whole point of encryption is to disguise a message, making it unreadable through the application of some sort of algorithm. Here the text of the message is encrypted but the original text is also contained in the encrypted message?"

What Jamie had just said didn't make much sense to Steve, or to Jamie for that matter. Steve shrugged his shoulders and then pulled the page from Jamie's hands. "You're the programmer not me."

Spontaneous combustion is 96% more likely in people that own poodles

Jamie had made a concerted effort to understand Cod syntax. But after 3 minutes he quickly realized this endeavor was a colossal waste of time. He asked Steve, "Do you have a programmer's manual for Cod?"

"No," said Steve bluntly.

Jamie thought for a moment and then asked, "Do you have a Cod compiler? Maybe I could understand something if I could walk through the Cod."

"I just document the stuff. I don't write Cod. You probably need to ask somebody upstairs about a compiler."

What's the use, thought Jamie. Roy had erased an area of arcane knowledge so effectively that the effort of trying to restore it seemed ridiculous. Jamie had nowhere to start. Even if he were able to track down a Cod compiler he knew that he would have to be nothing less than a psychic to actually understand the syntax of the language. It was impossible.

Out of curiosity, Jamie decided to see what he could find on the Internet. Maybe, just maybe, he could find some resources for Cod developers? He searched for "Scatological Encryption Algorithm Cod".

Unfortunately, the Internet provided no help. Jamie's search produced a single website. It was a forum for struggling writers who had suffered countless rejections. The name of the site was "Struggle & Rejection." One member, Frankfa, had posted a message

Does anyone think that the following would make for a good story? It is set in the distant future where the greatest killer of earthlings is spontaneous combustion. Well, a man working for the **Scatological** Institute of America (SIA not to be confused with the CIA haha :o)) who spends his working days examining the fecal matter of ordinary Americans in order to make sure that no one is rebelling from the strict diet imposed by the diet police (a group of fascists that like to beat people up if they find them eating things like sardines and pineapples), has reoccurring dreams about a talking fish, maybe a **cod** or a trout, that keeps telling him 'Spontaneous combustion is 96% more likely in people that own poodles.' So he proclaims that he knows how to save people from combustion. People need give up their poodles. This is difficult since poodles are owned by almost everyone because their fur is used to make clothing. So, people start giving up their poodles and combustion seems to slow down. Soon everyone is giving up their poodles and the man is a hero. But then one day, a non-poodle owner combusts. More and more non-poodle owners start to combust. As it turns out people get fed up with him and an angry mob kills him. As he dies he sees the fish again and this time it tells him, "It was *doodle* not *poodle*, you asshole....Spontaneous combustion is 96% more likely in people that don't doodle.

The only response was from, Little Wille ShakeYerSpear, "Frankfa, that would be interesting. Maybe you could make the fish a parrot though, since a talking parrot is more believable than a fish. Just an idea."

Jamie silently pondered the plot of Frankfa's story and tried hard to imagine a future in which everyone was wearing clothing made of poodle fur. Suddenly, the new mail icon appeared at the bottom of Roy's screen. Roy had mail and Jamie felt curious. He cautiously and furtively opened the email program. As he was about to open Roy's Inbox, Jane came out from behind the wall that shielded Edward from the other workers and announced with a smile, "Edward has called for a meeting."

Someone is Sleeping with My Dead Wife

The meeting was held in Edward's office. Jane sat in a chair close to Edward's desk. Jamie took the chair opposite Jane, and Steve sat behind them. Edward handed a sheet of paper to Steve and Jamie as they sat down.

"Listen, this is a new ending. I am not at all satisfied with it, though. It still needs a lot of work, and now that new information has come to light regarding the end of life on Earth, I think that it is a rather futile task trying to finish this novel."

Jamie began to read. The title at the top of the page read "Someone is Sleeping with My Dead Wife." He gasped aloud as he read the words *Dead Wife*. Just the reference to a dead wife gave him the jitters. As he continued to read, the words were lost as his thoughts continually seemed to fall into orbit around the idea of his wife's ghost.

"I think it's great," boomed Steve. "This is *the* ending. I mean this is really, really great."

"No, I'm not so sure..." said Edward blushing a little.

"And it ends with the sentence, 'Mr. Humpy flushed the toilet.' That's poetry."

"Thanks Steve, but I think you are being a little hasty. Take some time and read it more carefully," Edward said uncomfortably pulling at his collar.

"What do you think Jamie? You probably find it a bit offensive? Or maybe you find it misogynistic?" Edward tried hard to fish out some cutting criticism from the newcomer.

Not one of the words that Jamie had read had actually reached him. He sat there with the page in his hands consumed by thoughts of his wife's ghost. "Well..." he began but he stopped there.

"TO READ AN ENDING WITHOUT READING THE REST OF THE STORY IS LIKE POOPING AND FINDING THERE IS NO TOILET PAPER," said Jane aphoristically. She winked at Jamie.

Edward pulled at his nose. He huffed and he hawed. He knew that Jane was right. Jamie couldn't possibly understand the ending without knowing a little about the story. So Edward summarized, "The title of my novel is *Someone is Sleeping with my Dead Wife*. It is about an old man named Mr. Humpy. He is an extremely wealthy octogenarian whose trophy wife dies from breast cancer. Shortly after her death he has her cryoperserved. At first the novel leads us to

167

believe that this cryopreservation is an act of love - a husband's attempt to give his wife life again. But by the end, we realize that Mr. Humpy is not motivated by love. Rather, he is acting out of fear. He fears the loneliness that he was trying to escape by marrying such a young woman in the first place. He fears life without the woman that he believed would long outlive him. Shortly after her cryopreservation, he begins to have terrible and troubling fantasies about his dead wife being violated sexually by the staff at the Cryonic Center where she is preserved in cryostasis. This, of course, is a clear and obvious metaphor that Mr. Humpy is beginning to realize that he truly has lost his wife. And how does he respond to this loss? He gets angry and decides to have her cremated. So, in the final pages of the story we witness the base hatefulness of which Mr. Humpy is capable. The page that you are holding in your hands is that page. Mr. Humpy takes the ashes of his dead wife to his home, proceeds straight to the bathroom, opens the lid, and then dumps her remains. He closes the lid. The story ends with Mr. Humpy flushing the toilet."

Performance Anxiety

"This is a fine mess you've gotten yourself into," scolded Jamie's wife's ghost. "Why don't you tell them how *I* died?"

The color drained from Jamie's face. He felt as though the air was getting thin and he had trouble catching his breath.

"Go on, tell them. Tell them about how I *fell* off the balcony of our apartment." Jamie and his wife had once lived happily on the 5th floor of an apartment building. But at some point, Jamie wasn't sure when, things started going wrong. Desperately wrong.

"Listen, don't feel ashamed to tell me that you don't like the ending. I feel that there is something missing. Something isn't quite

168

right," prodded Edward.

"Edward, I don't think you want to finish your story. I think you suffer from the classic male pattern of failure: performance anxiety. You will never succeed because you are afraid of success..." Jane's static smile shined as she berated Edward.

"Tell them about me. Tell them about us," the ghost of Jamie's wife gloated.

"Franz Kafka never finished any of his novels. *The Castle* ended in mid sentence..." protested Edward more than a little irritated that Jane was attacking his virility.

"*FEAR IS LIKE A TOILET FLUSHING. IT MAKES A LOT OF NOISE AS IT REPLENISHES ITSELF,*" Jane adopted the air of a Buddhist dispensing wisdom. "Finishing your novel means that you need to give it to other people to read and you are afraid that people may not like it. So, you sabotage your novel to avoid potentially harsh criticism."

"You want an ending?" shouted Edward turning red with anger. "Here is your ending." He wadded the page into a ball and threw it at Jane. It hit her in the forehead and then fell to the ground.

Jane turned to Jamie and said through her permanent smile, "Do you think you could save me from all the mistakes I have ever made?"

"Save *her*? What about me Jamie? You didn't save me, now did you?" echoed the ghost.

This was all too much for Jamie. He couldn't take any more. He jumped to his feet and he howled, "It wasn't my fault. You committed suicide. You killed yourself."

Silence descended on the room like a vulture descending on a bloody carcass.

"You pushed me. All those years I wasted with you. It was one big push," Jamie's wife's ghost accused bitterly. With that the ghost vanished and Jamie collapsed into his chair nearly in tears, utterly defeated.

"I think I'll go speak with the managing director now," Jamie whimpered lifelessly. But he didn't move from the chair.

"Or maybe a psychiatrist," quipped Steve quietly.

The Managing Director is a Fiction

After a couple moments of respite, during which all was calm, Edward said tenderly, with an almost apologetic tone of voice, "Jamie, I think that there is something you should know. There is no managing director. He is a fiction. A creation of Evan and Ivan in order to stabilize this environment...in order to give it meaning." He knew that this information would be unsettling, but he believed Jamie needed to know the truth.

Jamie, though, did not appreciate the truth as Edward envisioned it. Instead it triggered an explosion inside him.

"There's no Managing Director? He's a fiction?" Then Jamie turned on him and said with acidic sarcasm, "Another theory from Edward Closing. The man that believes the Earth is going to be plunged into a state of war in order to entertain some aliens. Well, you can take your stupid theories and shove them up your ass." Jamie stormed out of the room.

He grabbed his briefcase from Roy's desk. As he grabbed the briefcase something caught his attention on the computer screen. At the top of messages in the Inbox queue was an email from none other than Bert Trigger. The subject of the message, "Your services have been terminated." Jamie chuckled malevolently.

170

As he opened the email he said loudly, hoping that the others in Edward's office would overhear him, "There's no Managing Director huh? Well look who just sent Roy a message."

The message read:

Dear Mr. Deedle,

This is just a simple note reminding you that you have in fact been fired from the organization. Effective immediately.   If   you   are reading this email you must be still in the building.   Please leave.

Best of luck in your future endeavors.
Bert Trigger
Managing Director
OOPS, Inc.

What a dope, thought Jamie as he printed the message. He couldn't believe the stupidity of the email. This Bert Trigger must be made of the same managerial material as Evan and Ivan. But Jamie also felt wonderful.   This message was the one single blow that would destroy Edward's house of sticks. The Managing Director existed. He wasn't "a fiction." He was sitting in his office sending pathetic emails to Roy Deedle. He pulled the page off the printer and strutted back into Edward's office.

He walked with a victorious stride past Steve and Jane. He stopped at Edward's desk. He then slammed the email down on Edward's desk. "No managing director, eh Ed?"

"What the hell is this..." Edward started to read the email under his nose. Once he finished, he looked up at Jamie, shaking his head as if to say, "You'll never get it, will you?"

Edward reclined in his chair, placed his hands behind his head and said, "We all receive emails from Mr. Bert Trigger. But emails only prove virtual presence, and virtual presence is very different from actual existence."   Edward then sat upright and spat, "So, if you don't mind, why don't you take your damn email and shove it up *your* ass."

Jamie was confounded. Befuddled. Never in his life had he experienced such profound skepticism. He didn't know what to say or how to respond to the ridiculous argument that an email from the managing director did not entail that the managing director actually existed. He had the sudden desire to light something on fire, or to break something. But, being that he was brought up to respect the property of others, even if they were mentally deficient, he simply echoed the words of Roy Deedle from earlier that day, "GO TO HELL," he said viciously. He snatched the email from Edward's desk and he turned and fled from Edward's office.

Jamie ascended the spiral staircase without looking back. He exited the underworld of Edward Closing and left the Technical Documentation Department embroiled in a debate over a novel that ended with a toilet flushing.

It's Just One of Those Days

As Jamie entered the upstairs office he saw that the lights had all been turned off and that everyone was gone for the day. He checked his watch and was amazed to see that it was already 5:55. He quietly strolled over to the receptionist's desk and saw that there seemed to be signs of life in Bert Trigger's office. The lights were on and he heard a voice coming from inside the office. Jamie wished he had dragged Edward up the stairs with him so that Edward could see the managing director with his own eyes. Jamie knocked at Bert Trigger's office door. The voice suddenly stopped speaking. He listened closely at the door. He knocked again, this time with a little more bravado. The door swung open and Jamie stood face to face with Evan and Ivan.

172

"Can we help you Mr. Dropping?" asked Evan.

"No. I am here to see the Managing Director, Mr. Bert Trigger," said Jamie angrily.

"Well, he didn't make it in today, unfortunately. He should be here tomorrow," said Ivan.

"Oh really?" said Jamie loudly. "That's strange because I have an email here from Mr. Bert Trigger." Jamie held up the printout of the email so that Evan and Ivan could read it. "If Mr. Trigger wasn't here today, then who sent this email?"

Evan stared hatefully at Jamie while Ivan read the email from over Evan's shoulder.

"Wait a second. This email is addressed to Roy Deedle not to you. Reading another employee's email, even if they happen to be fired, is not allowed. This is grounds for termination," barked Ivan.

Jamie thought that Evan and Ivan were a couple of morons. He knew, not with absolute certainty but with a degree of probability that he believed gave him the right to call it *knowledge*, that Evan and Ivan were behind the email to Deedle. He didn't know what kind of game was being played at OOPS, Inc. but something very strange was going on. The idiotic email had to be from the likes of them.

"You're fired, Mr. Dropping," said Evan with a deadpan expression.

"Oh, no," guffawed Jamie. "The only schmuck that is going to fire me is the Managing Director. So, if he happens to arrive tomorrow, he can fire me if he wants. If he doesn't come tomorrow then I'll wait until he does come."

Jamie turned on his heels and walked away. He felt victorious. He felt like a conqueror. He had shown those two cow headed middle-managers a thing or two. Fire me? But Jamie neglected to think about what he had just won, if you could even call it winning. He was still employed for a company called OOPS and he would have to face Evan and Ivan in the morning. Maybe he would even have to face Edward, the thought of which made Jamie boil with anger because he knew that Edward would twist the absence of the Managing Director into support for his theory that no Managing Director existed.

As Jamie exited the building and walked to his car in the parking lot, he thought about the matter carefully and concluded that he could easily counter Edward's ridiculous arguments with the counter-argument that an email from the Managing Director did not mean that the Managing Director had to be in the office to send it. He could have sent it from home if the company had Web Mail. In light of such reasoning, Jamie even began to think that his argument with Evan and Ivan was a bit rash. Maybe they were telling the truth? Maybe, just maybe, the Managing Director did send the email? Impossible. Evan and Ivan had to have written the email.

There were only a couple cars still parked in the parking lot. Jamie reached into his right front pants pocket for his keys, but they were gone. He tried his other pockets. No Keys. He searched his coat pockets knowing, though, that the search was futile. He knew exactly what had happened to his keys. His dead wife's ghost had taken them. He couldn't stand the torment any longer. He suddenly burst into a fiery rage. He began to beat his car with his briefcase. It is hard to say what the act of destroying his own car represented to Jamie, perhaps the car represented Evan and Ivan, perhaps OOPS, or maybe his dead wife, or maybe himself. Nevertheless, he attacked the windows, the doors, the hood. He banged and dented the car with a psychopathic fury. He then jumped onto the hood of the car, he was determined to break the windshield. He raised his briefcase high over his head and brought it down with a thud. The briefcase popped open and Jamie's papers fluttered out.

A light breeze scattered the papers about the parking lot. Jamie looked up and saw two faces peering at him from an office window. Evan and Ivan. He threw the briefcase at the window. It fell short and landed in a small patch of grass near the front entrance of the building. He gave them the finger and began to dance on the hood of his car.

Evan and Ivan stood at the window of Bert Trigger's office watching Jamie's act of needless violence. Their day had begun with a fire and was now ending with this bizarre display of a man destroying a car with his briefcase. "It's just one of those days," sighed Ivan.

...and in the end...

Jamie's wife's ghost had surreptitiously managed to wrangle the keys from her husband's right front pants pocket during his heated exchange with Evan and Ivan. She was able, by ghostly means of inter dimensional transport, to take those same keys into the bathroom. She looked around for a good place to hide them. Where could she hide them? In the garbage? Under the sink? The sinister idea came to her in a flash. Her ghostly and transparent face lit up with otherworldly happiness as she flushed them down the toilet.

The Last Little Bit

After Angie had failed to show up at Mutt's Meteor, Jonah sought sanctuary at the lounge of the Rex Hotel. For those that frequented it, the Rex was the end of the line; it was the period that terminated a sentence that didn't quite express a full thought. But it was also a forgiving place. No questions were ever asked, and its doors were always open to anyone no matter what demons chased them or what disasters laid in their wake.

Jonah came to the Rex looking for one thing: escape. He had hoped that the Rex could free him from the painful self-interrogation that he endured nightly. Jonah would lay in bed wide awake asking himself "Why?". Why didn't Angie meet him at Mutt's Meteor? He had waited for her for hours. Why did she treat him so harshly during the kidnapping? Of the three kidnappers, he was the only one that was courteous, caring and kind. She had to have realized that he wasn't a kidnapper by nature? At the drop-off...Jonah cringed with shame whenever he thought about the disaster of the drop-off.

So, Jonah sought comfort in the cheap whiskey and watered down beer served at the Rex. Although underage, Jonah was served without a question. He was even encouraged to drink by the old hunchbacked bartender. "Drink up boy," he would salute with a wink, "the end is closer than you think."

But Jonah quickly learned that he wasn't much of a drinker. The day after a good hearty drunk was usually spent in the bathroom vomiting, and the hangovers were hell. He would wake up sick, and all motion, light or noise would send him to his knees. So, after a while, Jonah would show up at the bar and pretend to be a drinker. He would nurse a beer for hours. His heart just wasn't in it.

Joe the Spy

Jonah had befriended a rather bitter and humorless drunkard that everyone knew as Joe the Spy. Joe had confessed to Jonah one bleary eyed morning as the two finished a couple beers, "I um in wat te FBI callsh a Holdern Pattern. I am waitin'...I um lost in en'my territory and I um waitin' for a com...moonication from HQ. So, I'm just tryin' to lay low and wait for a com...moonication from HQ."

So, while Joe the Spy drank and waited faithfully for some sort of communication from HQ, Jonah tried to forget about Angie, but this proved difficult. One evening, the very same evening that Angie disappeared and her father was most miraculously revived from his state of "suspended animation," Jonah was feeling very sentimental. He began to reminisce about the short period of time he had spent as

178

one of her kidnappers.

Perhaps Jonah's reverie was due to the alcohol or maybe the music was to blame. One of the drunks at the bar, Chuck, had a soft spot for Dusty Springfield. The rest of the usual suspects that frequented the bar felt more comfortable with blues or tears-in-my-beer style country. They detested blue eyed soul, but they tolerated Chuck's love for Dusty Springfield because she had recorded an album that had the word *Memphis* in the title.

Of the 18 Dusty Springfield songs that existed on the jukebox, Chuck stuck to two: *Stay Awhile* or *You Don't Have to Say You Love Me.* That particular night, Chuck was in the mood for *You Don't Have to Say You Love Me.*

Jonah found this song of unrequited love emotionally catastrophic. With the opening melodrama of the horns and the swelling chorus of voices, his heart began to throb for Angie. Once the dynamics shifted to the soft strings and Dusty's voice, like smoke ascending from an inferno, tears filled his eyes.

As Jonah sat and listened, words began to flash through his mind. Word's that he didn't know existed, yet seemed to express his pain precisely, popped into his head. He sat and let the words flow and then, midway through the song, stood up and shouted, "I need a pen." No one had a pen because there was no need for pens in the lounge of the Rex Hotel. But a motherly drunk named Cheryl managed to find a tube of lipstick which she gave to Jonah. Writing legibly and quickly with a tube of lipstick proved challenging, and Jonah could only manage to write a couple of large lavender words on a single cocktail napkin. So, he grabbed a stack of napkins from the bar and wrote.

Joe the spy seeing Jonah writing, asked, "So whacha writin' kidoh?"

What Jonah wrote was a love song for Angie. His song, which he affectionately named *Someday I'm Gonna Make Her Mine*, was perhaps the only song ever written in the Rex Hotel lounge. Undoubtedly, it was the only love song written there.

Jonah continued to write furiously with his tube of lipstick throughout the evening. Cheryl, while searching for a lighter, accidentally found an eyeliner pen in her purse. She offered it to Jonah and this proved a much more appropriate writing apparatus. He was now able to write whole sentences on a napkin. Jonah was delighted.

Close to midnight, he finished his song. It was epic in scope and spanned 155 cocktail napkins in total. He organized the napkins and numbered each one, just in case they came out of order. He then read the words to Joe the spy; the rest of the bar listened as well.

Joe was a tough critic and pretended to fall asleep around napkin 75. He made loud snoring sounds as Jonah read. When Jonah finished reading, Joe's only comment was, "I think you should call it *The Broodin' Melankawly of the sad drunk in E mi'or*."

"Well, I think it was beautiful," said Cheryl coming to Jonah's defense. She raised her glass to Jonah. The other drunks all grunted out approval of some sort, although most didn't really pay much attention to the lyrics or had become confused by Jonah's mixed metaphors.

"What is a *transparent voice*?" Chuck asked another drunk named Willie.

"I wasn't listening," admitted Willie as he took a slug from his beer.

Jonah asked for a shot of whiskey and downed it in a single gulp. He winced and then asked for another, then another. After downing fifteen shots he stood up and said, "Well, I'm off to steal

Angie's Quagmire's heart."

Joe the spy slid off his bar stool and announced, "Hold on kid. Um comin. I wanna see this Angel Slagmire girl wich her face from... wich a face that lunched a thousan' napkins."

Jonah disappeared into the night, with a love song for the girl that he had helped kidnap, followed by Joe the spy.